The Fear Before the Wife

Also by Georg Engel from K A Nitz:

Thy Neighbour's Wife

Sorceress Circe: A Berlin Romance

The Burden

The Fear Before the Wife

Georg Engel

K A Nitz
WELLINGTON

Die Furcht vor dem Weibe first published
in German 1899

ISBN: 978-0-473-28230-1

BOOK ONE

Mephisto:

Despise only reason and science,
The highest powers of mankind,
Let yourself only be strengthened
In deception and magic by the lying spirit,
Then I will have you for certain.

Faust, Part One.

The Dark Gate

No, no, not in the duel – that would not be enough of a joy for me, not enough air. – The knife in his neck so that I could see him falling, twitching on the ground, and my being delighted by it – that would be the fitting thing.

He would also have to be lying there on that fence, on the garden fence, nodding over the dark azaleas, exactly like my wife, my beautiful wife that I stabbed to death there.

But I will not arrive at this satisfaction.

I am imprisoned in this narrow room from which I can see through the solitary window only the garden which the patients themselves till. A high wall is drawn all around so that the madmen cannot escape, the lunatics. And among these pitiable men, I am held – I, the only healthy one, who is just a murderer.

If I only knew why they do not want to believe that of me.

It is true, I must surely have made a right tame, polite impression in the period of my brilliance, when I was still a university professor and teacher of literature. But what does that say? When an ape has committed a murder, a real murder, for which they beheaded an innocent man. And me, they do not want to concede to me the solitary beautiful and just act of my life.

Professor Barkentin has lost his mind. A year after his wedding. But he never murdered his wife. – That is what these men have bandied about, and over that I really could lose my mind again.

But still, I'm not giving up; I still hope that they will finally believe me.

Indeed the craftiest attempts have been set in motion to convert me from my ostensibly delusional idea. Recently Professor Wächter, the famed institute director, visited me.

It is strange that this man was my friend when I still possessed a home. How often he accompanied Lilli in song. It was a beautiful picture, to see this tall, broad shouldered man with the pale Christ's countenance sitting next to the slender, blond woman.

Had she also infatuated him?

Recently he visited me. He squeezed my hand and asked how it was going with me. I wanted to make fun of him, and pretended that a doubt had occurred to me in the preceding days as to whether I really did commit the gruesome act on my wife. He looked at me seriously, checked my pulse, then opened the window, and turned back to me after a while with a gentle smile on his beautiful saint's face.

"Look, my dear friend," he said, "I was expecting something similar all last week. Doubtless, an improvement in your condition has occurred. If you keep behaving so nice and demure now, go for walks in the garden diligently, and don't skip the cold showers which I decreed for you, then I believe you will have progressed so far that I can provide you in a few days with the last evidence."

"The last evidence?" I repeated with great obligingness, and had to laugh inwardly at what stupidity the famed Professor with the Christ's head went in with in my case.

"Yes," he responded, while he gauged me cautiously with his eyes. "Would you be able to receive the visit tomorrow – but, dear friend, now compose yourself – the visit of your wife, your real living wife?"

He suddenly fell silent, as if he feared having to expect a violent flare up from me. I, however, although the fury was already boiling up in me, held inconspicuously onto the table, and answered with a light bow, "Professor, I believe I will now withstand the sight."

He came up to me, even closer, and looked me again sharply in the face.

These strange dark eyes have some such odd quality of finding out, such a penetrating into the depths, as if they made chase like hounds on a hunt after the thoughts which were lurking behind my forehead. In such moments, I could throw myself on the man and throttle this Christ who so harried his patients.

But I composed myself. I smiled.

"So, tomorrow," he concluded meaningfully, and strode, elegantly and erect as ever, to the door. "You will lie down to sleep on time today!"

The next day, the monstrous thing really did happen. This vulgar, ridiculous deceit which they performed on me. With me, when I am no madman, but cleverer than all of them, with me, the murderer!

Towards 10 o'clock in the morning – my warder had just carried out the breakfast – Professor Wächter appeared, and asked me to step up to the window. He himself stood next to me, and did not let me out of his eye for a moment. Across the well tended gravel paths of the treeless, free space, a slender, blond female figure dressed in black appeared by the side of his first assistant.

That was meant to be Lilli, the dead Lilli, from whom, thank God, I freed the world.

She did not turn a glance to the place where I remained. Of course not. For if I had been able to examine the features of this lady, who admittedly resembled my wife superficially, then I would have immediately had to see through the crude deceit. Thus, however, the apparition glided past quick as thought – haha, probably to spare me. – And then Professor Wächter grasped my hand, and asked sympathetically, "Now, dear friend, isn't it true, you now see that your wife lives, and that you yourself were all the time only sick, and not depraved!"

Then I could not hold myself any longer.

I threw myself on the sofa, and began laughing loudly, ever louder and louder until the Professor had to surely notice that I had seen though his ridiculous tricks.

That miserable comedian!

How much sympathy, admirably acted sympathy, lay around his bearded mouth as he bent over the sofa to sit me up. Then he whispered again softly with a few assistants whom my laughing had enticed into the doorway. A few minutes later, I was alone with my warder.

They held me really to be so insane that they allowed themselves to play such a cheeky game on me.

And only one proof do I have, only one solitary proof which will convince them of my act of murder – the book which I am writing.

They are letting it happen unhindered; they probably believe I will thereby become calmer and it will serve for my amusement.

So I often sit for hours and write, my own prosecutor who delivers the glistening charges which must finally bring me to the scaffold.

"Just wait, just wait, all of you, when this book is first finished!"

I am not disturbed much.

Both my neighbours to the right and left, these poor, unfortunate creatures whose minds have gone astray, behave calmly. I believe they have respect for me.

One is a fat, massive butter merchant with coarse, puffed-up facial features and an almost completely bald head. The poor man – it is ridiculous to think of it – the poor man imagines he is a great Napoleon; a distant similarity in his handwriting is meant to have formed the basis for this delusion. He stands almost the entire day with his arms crossed by the window, and murmurs commands which he supposes he is giving to his marshals. He does not greet the other patients, he only sometimes acknowledges me by a light bow of his head. At the moment, he thinks he is located in the prison on St Helena. He shared that with me recently in the garden quite calmly and rationally.

My neighbour on the other side is the wife of a great merchant, a little, ugly, black-haired creature who is emaciated in every limb. Remarkable! This little ugliness considers herself a famous courtesan at whose feet the most well-known men, not just of our little coastal town, but of the entire land, have languished. She calculates her adulteries in the hundreds.

As if it were not enough for one!

Yes, it is enough for one. More than enough. Only that an avenger is not always found as I was, even if I am just a physically weak, dissipated man.

Hear it! Hear it, everyone! I am a murderer! I want to be one!

Now I am happy, now I am glad!
The chains jingle, the straw rustles.
The end is here, I am prepared,
Now he enters in hangman's clothes
And catches me — the day, it greys,
The scaffold is already erect outside.
Thank God! Now it's clear to all,
That I in truth was a murderer;
They sit there — it was no delusion.
"Good morning, gentlemen! I did it.
Now you finally believe what I committed,
That I stabbed my wife with passion.
Have thanks that you believe my work,
My only deed! — Here, hangman, my head!"

The Book

I

Sunshine lay all around the world; in the little coastal town you could here the distant roar of the sea. The swallows were shooting twittering into the high blue air, and I stood in the little elegant lady's room of the old gothic house by the market, standing between silk furniture, surrounded by breaths of a fine mignonette scent, opposite the wonderful blond girl who held her sparkling eyes lowered to her lap — there I stood, and worked away exultantly at the enormous edifice of my misfortune.

She held a sheet of white paper in her hand, on which my little, scrawled letters could be seen; her cheeks reddened, her lips moved gently.

Oh, you full red, womanly lips, you are accursed! Accursed! You lured me by your execrable whispering and stammering away from the even road on which I was strolling. You poisoned with your breath the air which seemed to me like a fresh greeting from nordic divinities. You breathed into the pure wells of my imagination a plague, stinking rubbish, sucked out of me with your red burning ardency the greatest treasure of a man, the joy in his profession, until I became loathsome to myself, a trifling birth, contemptible, unworthy among the others, until I became what I am now, a skeleton thrown out of the sea of life, a deadman, a nothing.

Oh you sweet, devilish lips, I hang on you again, I kiss you again timidly and shaking like the first time — but then I step back from you shuddering and call over you the ghastliest curses for eternity. Contemptuously may the worm that now draws near to these modern messengers of love creep back, a loathing of all creatures!

And yet — I loved you!

***

She raised her dark eyes up to me.

Something like astonished admiration lay in them, as if she were examining in me a creature from a higher world unfamiliar to her.

"Yes, I found this poem in the book that you left behind with me yesterday."

"You have read it?"

She fell silent for a moment. On her cheeks, a wonderfully rosy shimmer ignited as if the morning sun were glimmering over our wide snowy landscapes.

"Yes," she finally said firmly.

A sweetly timid silence arose again between us. I looked out past her gleaming blond hair through the window to the old market, over which the threads of the sun were drawing past in the light.

But she did not stir. She was quite absorbed in what lay there before her, in what I meant.

Certainly, certainly, that was the woman, the long-desired whom invisible forces had nominated for me, that would complete and fill me out in my essence.

Suddenly she stood up, and turned towards me.

Her breasts rose under the simple, black, close fitting, and yet so dressy garment. The entire being of this remarkable creature seemed to be binding itself into the question which it now wanted to direct at me.

I stood before her as if I were rooted not to the earth, but to the distant cloud land that my imagination, the imagination of a poet, had created over decades.

"Who is this blond girl whom you speak of in your marvellous, gripping poem, doctor?"

"You – you, Lilli!"

"Me? Really?"

Over her proud white countenance, one of those strange regal smiles again passed which had already put me in a whirl so often. That remarkable swaying and trembling befell me again before this woman, and I was overcome by the uncertain, miserable feeling which all men surely experience who do not know women, do not know their company, have only dreamt and imagined a woman until then. From this feeling, I became most miserable.

"And you talk in your poem with a princess, yes, with a queen, doctor?" she said still in her proud pose, but with a fleeting smile. "Oh, but not – but not me, the simple daughter of the merchant Karström, whom you outclass so infinitely in everything? Yes, you know, sometimes I think that these literature lessons which you have given me since my return, out of incomprehensible kindness, must secretly be a torment for you. And now — no, it pleases me anyway, it makes me very proud, now you are paying homage to me so unthinkingly?"

At the same time, she stepped once quickly through the little room, erect and majestic like one of the white images of gods which are sculpted up in the northern capital.

I stood there, silent, motionless, with whirling, stormy thoughts. It seemed to me constantly as if I would have to collapse crying and worshiping before this wandering beauty.

Oh, if I had never left the seclusion of my study, the shadow of my fond books!

When she paused before me again, something like a stormy desire lay in her proud face. She looked at me, deep and enquiringly; I could spot my own reflection in her sparkling blue eyes.

Then she gave me her hand with a certain wildness. She herself it was who, with a strong motion, led her fingers to my mouth.

She wanted to be kissed.

It passed through my limbs like a jolt. I felt her by me, ever closer, a wild, stormy shaking was running through this slender body, she bent down, leant her head with its metallically gleaming, blond hair on my chest, and lifted her gently opened lips up to me.

Then it broke over me.

Fervour, streams of fire, unconsciousness! It was something like the greatest happiness, the wildest wistfulness – but then, in the midst of all this quivering lightning, a terrible vision.

Already at the time of the first, blessed kiss!

I saw my study with the old bookcases, I saw my mother, the little, white-haired woman, how she waited for me with her brother, old Captain Holm, in our cosy mariner's home, and suddenly felt a mad, indescribable desire for this calm.

"Do you really love me, Karl?" asked the quivering voice of the beautiful woman I was holding in my arms. "Tell me, otherwise I won't be able to believe it."

"Yes, yes, I love you! Only you! Lilli, you don't know how much all my spirit has pursued you this entire year. Through all my work, your image swayed back and forth before me; I could find no peace anymore, neither with my mother, nor with my students at the university. When I told you of Werther's Lotte, I saw you, when I was explaining to you that gloriously sprawled out phantom of a woman in Faust, then it was you, you, Lilli, to whom I stretched out my arms, to whom all my verses were applied. And only one thing is incomprehensible to me, how you, the celebrated, wondrous daughter of the wealthy merchant, of the millionaire, could choose, from among all the landed people and officers who idolise you, me, the – I know – awkward academic so inexperienced in all worldly things."

Then she rose, examined me again from head to foot and threatened me with a, this time really blissful, smile.

"You, dear," she just said, "I'm so proud of you – of you, yes, of course our entire town is proud of you, your dear educated head!"

She leant towards me again, and caressed my dark hair with her small hands.

When she raised her arm, this statuesque motion which could have inspired a sculptor delighted me.

And then a scene followed whose fearful emotion still adheres to me today in painful recollection.

I was suddenly sitting in the silk fauteuil behind the red damask curtains which enclosed the old gothic window, and had the beautiful woman on my knee. Both her glorious arms lay around my neck, that wondrous budding bosom close to my chest. All the love, melting devotion, desire, the entire crackling and fizzling fire of youth in which the virginal bashfulness burns to ashes.

And me — an icy fear ran through me, still ripples through me today, pricking me like sharp needles of ice. I sat there, overawed, unfamiliar with this fervour. In my dreams, in my poetry, I had visualised the woman in my imagination as gleaming white, my intoxicated senses had paid homage to her yearningly, and now — what was it? The reality frightened me, betrayed me.

I did not know how to respond. In the midst of our caresses, I thought, while a contradictory, nagging fear ran through me at the same time, of precious books, of long vanished words from my mother. Only not of that which was pulsing and fevering so close to me here.

She must have finally noticed. Taken aback, she lifted her head, her lips moved as if she wanted to ask something, but she did not vocalise it.

I will never forget the strange expression in her eyes, as if she were observing me in this terrible pause. Then she rose, tidied her hair, and stepped to the window.

Oh, how wonderfully well proportioned this figure was!

She bent down, and picked up the sheet of paper which had slipped from her a short while ago and on which my poem was written.

Salvation! Salvation!

Those fervently loving words guided us both onto a different track.

She held the little sheet before her, and read. Her voice sounded silvery light, she herself slowly sparked to the homage which was offered to her and which also explained at the same time my entire unhappiness.

The poem read:

Prayer

O, Mahadb, good God of the earth,
You who in unending weaving
Encompass the world,
Penetrate and fill it
With streaming power of becoming
So that nothing is except you
And in you,
You who enlivened the good well
And fashioned the bad badly,
So that there is eternal change
And man strives for completion,
You also gave man woman — —
The still unconquered glorious woman,
Laid her in his arms
So that she, with her kiss,
Awoke all that is tender in him,
Sympathy with her weakness

And the active desire to help.
A string however
Of your thousand toned harp,
You drew through the woman's breast
So that there everything
That man created rings again,
Deep and emotional,
A trembling echo of his deeds and works
So that in quiet rest,
He'll hear himself in the woman.

So your eternal commandment!
Why now, you discerning, kindly God,
Do you forget me alone?
Why am I lacking
The gleaming sovereign crown of man.
Just me?
And why does she twinkle dazzlingly,
A fearfully charming diadem
On the blond locks of the one
Whom I must follow irrevocably,
Follow eternally and silently
Bow when she goes past.

Princess, queen, speak to me
One solitary word!
One solitary!
Speak if you have noticed me
In the corner,
In the deep shadows,
When you draw past radiantly
And invisible spirits singing to you
Are carrying the rustling train.

***

Salvation!

As she was reading this, a jubilation arose in her breast, admiration radiated from her eyes, we rushed towards each other, and held ourselves embraced. One thing led to another; the spiritual bond, the poetry, had shackled us together again.

"Tomorrow I'll tell my father everything," she whispered.

"And I my mother, my dear mother," I replied swiftly.

She offered her hand to me again, this time I led it to my lips; when she felt my kiss, she shut her eyes.

Then I was outside, walking across the market, and turning around again.

No, it was no dream; there lay the old gothic house, the venerable edifice, which for me and the companions of my boyhood constantly formed the object of venerable admiration. And above in the window, the glorious figure still remained, the daughter of this princely merchant, whom I had won.

Oh, there was brightness in me, brightness and jubilation. I walked home like an intoxicated man to inform the little woman in the cosy mariner's house of my fortune.

II

"So it is Lilli Karström?" my mother murmured half to herself.

She was standing in her old, black silk dress, the prayer book under her arm, and I was helping her to place a turkish shawl for churchgoing around her shoulders. It was Sunday, and the bells of St Mary's were calling loudly through the town.

Over the even face of the little woman, no joyful gleam passed as I had expected, she did not exult, she did not take me in her arms, she did not bless me. Her spirit seemed to remain strangely untouched by the sudden announcement.

She stood, buttoned up her black silk gloves, and her faithful grey eyes which had watched tirelessly over my childhood, which had read every secret desire from my soul, strayed past me, and riveted firmly on the bookcases by the wall.

I suddenly became aware of how cosy this old mariner's house was, how clean these thin, wrinkled hands constantly kept it, how contentedly and fulfilled I had lived next to the small woman until then.

"Mother," I said suddenly to wake her up.

"My dear, dear boy," she whispered, deep in thought.

My mood became ever more apprehensive, I recognised quite distinctly my mother's thoughts; she was thinking that I would be disentangling myself by my engagement from all my old habits, so that a chasm would open up between the two of us, and of whether my fastidious, sensitive nature was also capable of adjusting itself to all the unfamiliar things which would now close in on me.

"Mother," I called again anxiously.

At this moment, the regal girl from the gothic house by the market was completely forgotten. It seemed to me constantly as if I had to beg for forgiveness singly and alone from this old woman for some wrong I had committed.

"Don't you share my joy at all then?" I stammered.

"Oh, of course, Karl," she now answered quickly. "It just happened so quickly for me. But God will bless you, and your father in heaven will pray for you."

With that, she embraced me, and — oh, it seemed so sound to me in this embrace.

Then a fearful hurry came over my mother. She grasped my hand and examined me from all sides as if she wanted to spot something new on me. "Isn't she very proud?" she inquired while she looked me uncertainly in the face. "Will she be able to get her bearings in my small circumstances?"

"Oh — of course, mother — of course."

"And is she fond of you, Karl?" she now asked, almost with trembling fear, and squeezed my hand spasmodically. "Is she fond of you?"

This unease became my own. Was it not as if my mother, my best friend, doubted the inclination of the other?

But why? Why?

Did it seem really so impossible that a beautiful woman could feel drawn to me?

A certain sensitivity took possession of me. I know now that I was a fool at the time, and responded half aggrieved to my mother, "Calm down, mother, I'm quite convinced that Lilli is very devoted to me, yes, that she holds me in high regard."

"High regard?" the little woman repeated slowly. And then a new question came hastily, "Is she good, do you think, my boy — is she really good?"

"Yes, yes, good and noble."

I lied, spoke consciously the untruth to comfort my mother. For I knew nothing of Lilli, had never seriously tested her innermost character. She had just been beautiful to me, proud, the glorious woman, the phantom from the cauldron who bewitched my mind, who tempted me irresistibly away from my scholarly room.

"Then much has been won," my mother then whispered, sighing, while she pressed her hymn book to her breast, "if she is good. — Now you must bring her to me soon, your bride, your dear bride. — See, my heart aches so, my boy."

A few large tears were running over her thin cheeks. And again it seemed to me as if I had brought into our little house a wrong, a sin never to be put right again.

"But we will be very happy, we three," I consoled the little woman half unconsciously, "won't we?"

"Yes, yes — we will — be very happy," she repeated quickly to me.

Then she freed herself from me, and suddenly broke open her hymn book.

It was a superstition.

On all important occasions, my mother opened this book of edification, and the first verse which her eye fell on, she considered an omen, a reporting of fates, a divine revelation.

Instinctively, a certain tension also took possession of me.

"Well, mother?" I asked, stepping closer.

She had settled down at my writing desk. Now she hurriedly shut the black velvet covers.

"Oh, nothing," she answered with a forced smile on her kind face and avoided looking at me. "You can't take anything from it. – No, no, nothing really. – You can be quite unconcerned, my boy."

With that she rose – always hasty and fitful as if she were forcing herself to forget something.

A little spot of dust was found on my black coat. She wiped it away painstakingly.

Then she went, and left me alone.

***

Here I was interrupted.

The wife of the great merchant in the next cell, who imagined herself to be a courtesan, wanted intentionally to disturb me. She was annoyed, she had been aggrieved for days that I sat and wrote so untouched by her charms.

She thought to avenge herself for it.

She crept to the side wall, scratched at the wallpaper, and sung from time to time lewd songs.

Yes, just sing – sing; I take care not to react to it in any way; for if you leave your furies unheeded, you calm down soonest of all.

You should have memorised that, worthy Professor Wächter, you should have learned that from me.

Yes, just sing, sing. Your songs fit the images which I write. You recall for me all the lustful, baneful things which destroyed me.

Just sing, sing!

III

When my mother had left me, I threw myself on the chaise longue and endeavoured to conjure up the old kaleidoscopic, numbing dreams of love in which I had previously indulged.

I had always seen a superhuman, white glittering, glorious woman who bent down to me, and in whose kisses I slowly passed away.

But remarkably, I had never thought to subjugate this goddess, to make her mine, to shackle her to me for ever.

No, no, I actually lived constantly in hope, in yearning, ardent expectation.

And now I was soon to take possession.

Ridiculous – I began suddenly to mock myself for cherishing such strangely brooding, hairsplitting thoughts. It was all decrepit.

Lilli loved me, and I – now, I worshipped her, and possession should be the greatest. The greatest happiness for a man.

Yes, truly, I was happy, happy and enviable. – If only the time would soon be up. If only all the new, unaccustomed things soon lay behind me, if only I had already penetrated into all the mysteries which still lay darkly before me.

And again the fear began to plague me that I had up to now engaged myself so little with women.

All of my students were in many things more of a connoisseur than I. Often I had listened to their conversations with timid curiosity. For my delicate, weak body had previously excluded me from a great part of their enjoyments.

And now this full, mature woman for me.

A peculiar unease befell me. It would certainly have been fitting, if I had sought out Lilli around this time. From the church, it was already striking twelve. And yet an unconquerable anxiety deterred me from this visit.

No, no, not to her!

If her love were to embrace me again as ardently as the day before, and if I, on the other hand, were to stand before her as dull, impassive, and unresponsive as in that appalling moment.

No, no, not to her! An impregnable fear before her blossoming beauty shook me — and next to it — it seemed like madness — a burning desire for her.

Then there was a knocking on the door.

"Come in!"

And in stepped old Captain Holm — my mother's brother — took off his seaman's cap and looked around the room a little at first as if he could not discover me.

"Well, where are you then, my boy?"

I cleared my throat. Then he noticed me.

"God — what are you doing there?" he grumbled. "A bridegroom doesn't loll about so!" Then he came up to me with both hands, beaming. "But I congratulate you, Karl, I congratulate you. — Look, it is prudent that you don't want to establish a house now, very good. And for Lilli Karström, that is proper; money is there, another devil that I put up with. Well, is she mightily besotted with you, the little girl?"

I did not know why this question threw me into confusion. The old sea dog's fresh, earthy approach seemed so justified to me. A girl madly in love with the man of her choice, body craving after body, and yet it already seemed clear to me now that such a relationship between me and Lilli did not exist.

But why not?

My entire, failed life would bring me the answer to that.

"God damn, Karl!" my uncle cried, having left me a while in this brooding, "now that's enough. This being a bookworm must stop now. Be happy, boy, that you are now receiving such a nice, lovely thing so softly into your arms. Well? Right?" He stood up, spat, and walked with broad seaman's strides up and down the room.

"Now of all things, strip out of that black preacher's coat. – That thing has for me something of the musty saintliness about it. – And then to the tailor, and have something properly cavalier, something magnificent made which just makes you say wow. And then send flowers every day – well, the son-in-law of Karström can do such a thing. – And then companionship and sled rides, and strenuously smothering with kisses behind the curtains so that little girl also sees that she has received a fellow."

"Uncle – –"

"Understand me right, Karl – I mean it well with you, I tell you, girls whistle afterwards at all your learning. And such a female, when she is just married, would rather see you in a palpable brothel than that beautiful poem. Well? Right?"

He spat again, and threw a book I had been reading scornfully onto the writing desk.

I followed it with my eyes. An inner voice was whispering to me that the old, rough man there was tackling one of the black spirits which sat on my path to strangle me.

Then — was it an illusion? — No, it was true and veracious, I then heard Lilli's bright voice on the stairs. Hasty steps neared.

Every dark ghost had flown away, fluttered off. I felt like my heart was pounding with joy.

But yes, yes, and a thousand times yes. It was love, the desire was just pulsing so. I loved her. All my fears were phantasms, imagination.

IV

My mother had met Lilli and her father at church. My girl had been emphatic about wanting to visit me for the first time and even amidst my books.

I had the evening before asked her father in writing for permission to marry her.

Now she stood there, fresh and elegant in the black dress with which her blond hair contrasted so lovingly, and looked full of astonishment and admiration around my narrow scholarly room.

"Yes, that is his room," my mother said with a wistfully proud smile, while she cautiously pushed a chair towards the merchant Karström.

"Here we have really spent some happy hours. I think too," she added softly – "he will have difficulty becoming accustomed to another room."

And now came something so agreeable, dear, cosy, whose silvery sound echoes even today – after so many years – joyfully in my heart.

"He shouldn't either!" Lilli exclaimed confidently. "Right, Karl, don't you think? We will of course stay here in this cosy scholar's home, which I cannot imagine being any more beautiful. – And if I have my way," – with which she took the little woman's hand with an ingratiating gesture – "then your mother will stay too."

"Really? – Really, young lady?"

My mother set her eyes for the first time fully on my bride, as if she wanted with this look to fathom the innermost being of the stranger, to read my entire fate from her features.

"Oh, that would really be my heart's desire," she added then almost pleading, "if I could remain close to my boy. – I could even then move up to the second floor."

I stood completely entranced. I had not pictured my future so benignly.

"So, done!" Lilli confirmed with her bright voice, and offered my mother her hand anew. "But why do you say 'young lady' to me and not Lilli?"

"Oh God!" – The little woman smiled a little bashfully. "But if you wish, then with all my heart."

"I would like to be able to call you mother," my bride spoke softer, "my own — —"

"Yes, she is no longer alive," the merchant threw in-between, sitting stiffly on the chair, his top hat in his hand.

I constantly had the feeling as if the entire circumstances of his future son-in-law appeared to the distinguished looking, grey blond gentleman to be too narrow, too limited. But it had a perfectly distressing effect on me as Uncle Holm now, who had been standing there with legs apart, and examining the two new relatives in depth, suddenly entered the conversation unabashed.

"All dead? Ah, that is a pity," he consoled. "When the many joys of families had now arrived, pity."

"Yes, a great pity," the merchant cut him off.

Then he rose, laid his hand a little patronisingly on my shoulder, and said rapidly and clearly, quite in the tone of a great businessman who wants to illuminate a business matter in the brightest way, "So, my dear doctor, you have my consent. I hear in general that you are mentioned with esteem in your subject. Now, well, I am less capable of judging that. My daughter has also been accustomed since I can remember to a lot of independence, so that my will would from the outset carry less weight than her heart's choice. I would like to now ask you to seek me out tomorrow at midday in my office at the shipping company, so that we can discuss there all the details somewhat more in depth. You understand me. Apart from that, our desires probably coincide regarding a properly quick wedding, right?"

"Yes," my bride spoke joyfully, while she looked steadily at me.

Involuntary, my heart pounded, I bowed in a daze.

The merchant waved his hat casually. “Now, and if you really are sticking to your decision to want to remain living in this mariner’s house,” he concluded measuredly, “then allow me to be able to furnish these rooms fittingly. Thus you will be welcome to me, dear son!”

He offered me as a sign of endorsement once more his finely gloved fingers.

At this moment, Lilli threw herself suddenly on my chest. Oh, how softly her limbs huddled against mine; an agreeable warmth penetrated me, and through my every vein trickled instantly the joyful consciousness that she had disentangled completely from her father and wanted to belong only to me — to me.

How beautiful she was. How strange the affect she had among these old bookcases.

“No, no, Karl,” she whispered quickly, “don’t look so timid. Papa must not disturb all these treasures. Where you dwell, there everything will remain unchanged. You will only receive me into it. The young Mrs Barkentin. Will that be so difficult for you?

A surge of blood streamed into my brain. — “You dear thing,” I stammered enraptured, and with a sudden, wild fervour, I embraced her, and squeezed her close.

Remarkably, here, surrounded by my books, the original self-consciousness slipped from me more and more. Yes, with a certain pride, I even felt my own intellectual superiority.

Ha, this feeling was precious.

In me coalesced the knowledge of entire generations, the cultural work of many centuries; I was the well from which this proud, regal creature now leaning on me so devotedly wanted to scoop thirstily; I was the giving, the streaming source which understood how to guide the precious water over these hot lips.

Did she not stand there as if she now already awaited ardently such a drink?

And I, lunatic fool, really believed that at the time.

"Come, Karl," she then said joyfully while squeezing my hand furtively. "Now introduce me to your books. What is that there?"

"That's Homer."

"Yes, those in the pig leather, they are quite dear," Uncle Holm, who had volunteered as chaperone, threw in between.

My bride nodded to him.

"And these large sheets of paper here on the desk?" she asked further.

"Yes, that is his new work," my mother explained to the merchant meaningfully.

Oh, the poor old woman meant of course that the entire world must listen to every word of mine.

"His new work?" my bride repeated raptly, while she burrowed curiously in the large sheets.

Good God, this penetrating interest subjugated me to her, made her slave out of me.

And she was so glorious. A sunbeam falling through the low windows played luminously in her golden hair.

She wanted everything concerning me explained. Excited and inwardly exalted, we walked beside each other, always followed by Uncle Holm.

After the books, she examined the portraits on the wall, then the photographs of my university friends and colleagues. She wanted to know in depth about individuals who were standing particularly close to me.

There especially was my former lecturer and current colleague, Professor Wackermann, the portrait of whom infused the greatest interest in her.

"So this dear old gentleman will associate with us?"

"Certainly, he visits me daily."

"Oh, I have heard several of his public history lectures. It was magnificent. He speaks like a poet, like an aficionado. We ladies were all completely intoxicated. — Really, it must be beautiful to be allowed to live in these circles. — Just see, Karl, what an enthusiast's face your friend has."

"Now probably," Uncle Holm rasped. "But his trousers cannot be distinguished from his jacket. And his maidservant must dress him in the morning; isn't that right, Karl?"

Here Lilli laughed over her entire face. "Do you also know that you are a splendid old man?" she asked ingratiatingly, and stretched her hand out to the old captain with a quick motion.

"Well, and I like you too, young lady, quite colossally," the seaman responded, and shook my bride's hand as if he wanted to break off the little fingers for all time. "You are a fine wench, as they say. And if Karl is sensible, then he will sit down now diligently in his trousers, and fix you up as wife of a professor. For such a role belongs to you."

My bride looked at me. In her eyes swam so much tenderness, so much strangely shimmering hope that I was intoxicated by it.

I pressed the glorious woman against myself, close and tight, and said bravely and decisively, "Yes, Lilli, that I will. I will deploy all my powers, strain every thought to make you happy."

"That I am," she whispered blushing, "I am even without that, Karl."

More and more ardently, I embraced her, and looked over her shoulder at the bookcases by the wall.

I was a fool. I was an idiot.

For unseen by me, a little black devil sprang down from each volume, countless of them, until the floor swarmed black, and they towered up printed paper between me and the woman of my choice, higher and higher, towering up more and more until a partition wall had been erected between us. A paper wall which separated us.

That was my life.

V

Time flew. I still have unclear, vague memories of the months which lay between my engagement and our wedding.

Disengaged and absentminded, as they emerge for me from the blue abysses, I want to set them down here.

***

It was a rainy autumn evening. I was called to my father-in-law. I had to seek him out in his office at the dockyard.

The rain drove ringing against the panes of my scholarly room. My mother only let me go out in the weather with misgiving. She thoughtfully carried my gumboots over to me, and turned my coat collar up.

"Take care of yourself, boy," she warned.

Just as I wanted to set off, Professor Wackermann appeared in the door. He noticed under his blue glasses, which contrasted strangely with his smooth shaven, friendly countenance, immediately that I was departing.

"Good evening, Karl."

"Good evening, dear Wackermann."

"Off to your bride?"

"Unfortunately not. Only to my father-in-law."

"So? Does no harm. I'll stay with your mother. Well, how's it going with the folksongs?"

"Excellently. I've already found two new ones again. From up by Rügen."

"Really. – Well, I'd like to have a peek straightaway. The captain's wife will show me, eh? Now go on your way."

"But don't hold it against me, dear friend."

"God forbid – just go, my son."

"Well, then goodbye."

As I opened the door, the cosy picture struck me fully in the eye once more.

The scrawny, lanky man with the delicate, refined enthusiast's countenance, to which the grey brown hair hanging down simply lent something almost venerable, was sitting at my writing desk. The low work lamp was letting its circle of radiance fall brightly onto his forehead. His blue glasses seemed even darker than usual.

Thus he remained, and sank himself eagerly to the newly found folk tales. Around his mouth, a trace of delight played as if he were sipping precious, warming wine.

And next to him was the small, white haired woman looking down contentedly at her son's work.

I closed the door quite gently, as if I were frightened of disturbing them both.

***

Work was continuing at the dockyard.

A fine, penetrating rain was trickling down in the wide yard and soaking the ground.

From the river, white, smoky mists were swelling up, mixing with the vapour of the chimneys, and through all the haze gleamed the red fires of the flues hissing and moaning under huge bellows.

Booming hammer blows echoed throughout the premises.

I strode through long corridors, and was finally led to the private room of the merchant.

In the small room, there was only a delicate, almost too elegant, writing table, and on the wall hung a life-size oil painting of my bride.

When my father-in-law noticed me, he immediately discharged two engineers who were standing in front of him with plans and drawings.

"Excuse me – tomorrow, gentlemen."

Then he rose, and shut the door which led to the adjoining draughtsmen's hall behind them himself.

I sat there in my drenched overcoat, and followed his movements with uneasy tension.

What did he want from me?

He sat down behind his desk opposite me. Then he cleared all sorts of papers and books to the side as if he did not know how it should begin.

"Well?" I finally asked after a pause.

Then he lifted his grey eyes sharply up at me, and examined me as if he were seeing me for the first time that day.

I was getting hot.

The businessman seemed to be seeking something hidden behind me.

"I have had you called, dear son-in-law," he finally began with his accustomed restraint, "because a few days ago, I — — but you must not by all means misunderstand me —"

The sweat slowly rose on my forehead.

"Now, we are both men," he continued cold-bloodedly. "I heard a few days ago from one of my captains an allusion to your blessed father's end which I did not want to leave undiscussed. — Do you understand me now?"

Pale as a corpse, I suddenly had to cover my face, my feet turned ice cold, I stared at him, and only moved my lips a little.

This borderless, indescribable rawness robbed me of speech.

The merchant also rose, a little bashfully. With lowered head, he stood before me as he continued speaking, "I understand quite well that it must be painful for you, as his son, to give me information about this. — But by the same token," — he shrugged his shoulders — "is it true that your father died in a fit of mental derangement?"

Then I sprang up.

Everything was blurring before my eyes, it seemed to me as if I felt every drop of blood streaming individually and pulsating through my neck and brain. A strange shaking flew over my knees. I knew that I was master of my destiny for the last time.

And then — then my erratic glance fell on the portrait on the wall.

How entranced I stared up at it.

My eyes remained riveted to the bare arms of this beautiful, reclining body, and the red, voluptuous mouth, whose cosy warmth I had felt so often, seemed to bend down to me.

On the slave, the brand of the owner was imprinted once and for all.

"Now," the merchant asked, "may I count on an answer?"

"Certainly," I blurted, and almost crushed the edge of the writing desk in my hands. "You heard correctly, my father succumbed in fact to a brain ailment."

"So?" came prolonged from the lips of the merchant.

He made a motion of regret as if an already concluded business would be dissolved again by it.

I do not know why I was miserably beset by an almost mad fear of losing forever the beautiful woman smiling down at me so lovingly from the wall there.

No, no, I could not do without her, this loved one whose ample, consummate physicality my imagination enthused over.

I straightened up tautly and spoke crisper and firmer than before, "Did your informant also tell you that my father at the time commanded a ship coming from China?"

"Certainly — why?"

"Because he left here as a healthy man and only fetched a creeping fever there."

"Ah, and you want to say by that — — ?"

"That for me, no reason for fear exists health-wise as you seem to assume. I wish you had spared me this interview. — I would rather not pursue it any further."

A pause arose.

You could distinctly hear the thundering of hammers and the short thrusting of the machines.

My father-in-law strode once quickly about the small room, then he made a fitful, decisive movement, stopped before me, and slowly offered me his hand.

"It's okay," he started with difficulty and yet somewhat friendlier, "forgive me, dear son, but I only have the one child. And in all points of life, the utmost clarity is the most salutary thing. But it is better so. — As I said, forgive me, and may we see each other again soon."

He bowed his head measuredly, and looked to the door of the adjoining hall.

I was dismissed.

Outside the rain drizzled down heavier. As I hurried across the yard, I heard distinctly how the river threw small waves at the quay. A cold flurry of rain ran into my face.

And yet I was seething hot. Raging in me were two thoughts, two demons mutually who had to destroy each other, kill each other off.

The appalling, threatening ghost of the dead man, which I had as a boy already thought of with horror, emerged before me. I saw him on his ship, leaning pale as a corpse against the mast, gliding to me like the flying Dutchman to fetch the happiness from me. And alongside it, I was consumed by a dashing, mad desire for the kisses of the beautiful woman they had wanted to steal from me. So stormily, so longingly, I had never desired before.

I vigorously threw the dockyard gate shut.

And behind me, I heard for a long time yet the surging of the waves like the hoarse voices of water spirits scoffing at me from behind.

***

It was an hour later.

I was sitting in my study, leaning back in my rocking chair.

Professor Wackermann was still there.

And next to me, nestled close to me so that I could feel her curly hairs on my forehead, could sense the warmth of her body full of foreboding, sat Lilli, who had paid a visit to my mother that evening, and had waited for me.

I rocked gently while clasping her hand, and the more intimately and deeper we looked each other in the eye, the greater the fear I felt of this dear creature who belonged to me, this glorious woman, being able to slip away from me.

Deep, trembling desire seized me. I had the mad wish that my soul would melt and merge completely into this wonderful body. Oh, this desire was so tormenting and yet so painfully enjoyable.

A pleasant twilight reigned in the small room. The floor lamp illuminated only the figures of the Professor and my mother who sat attentively opposite him at the table with her knitting.

And with his dashing, somewhat elevated intonation, the old gentleman was still reading from my collection of folksongs.

From time to time, he looked up, shook his head with inner satisfaction, and murmured with a laughing mouth, "Beautiful, beautiful — really beautiful —."

Once, however, he interrupted himself, and turned directly to my bride. "Now, what do you think of this work of your boy's, hey?"

Furtively she squeezed my hand even tighter, but she replied to my friend plainly, "Oh, these old ballads have something of the mysterious about them for me. You don't know whether you should be delighted or scared by them."

"Good God, you're right there," the Professor cried, visibly astonished over her answer — "be delighted or scared — hm." Then he nodded to us, and continued in his reciting aloud again.

My mother brought a few glasses of tea. Outside the rain was clattering against the panes. The wind was moaning audibly through the streets. But we were cosy.

Lilli leant her cheek on mine, and remained calmly in this position. Oh, it was the first time that she had cuddled up to me in that way. We sat quite still next to one another. And inwardly I pleaded to her, "Stay with me. Don't leave me."

But I spoke no word. And yet it was as if she had understood me.

More and more remarkably, submissive and devoted at the same time, her steel blue, gleaming eyes lost themselves in my own.

Only she was present.

Only she.

We gently rocked away, and my mother raised her eyes from her work, and smiled softly over at us.

VI

My memories always stand still before my wedding. Agonising days were coming.

I could not release my spirit from the thoughts which my father-in-law had called forth by his question.

What if the miserable inheritance were now bequeathed to me? If the furies which would whip me before them were already coming racing through the air?

Strangely — now — here in the madhouse, where I know that I cannot go mad, that I, by a marvellous ointment, am immune to it, now I could smile over this boyish unease.

But at the time, it was tormenting, appalling.

The image of my father became more and more distinct to me, and drove me away from my work. Even Lilli noticed my unease. For since the businessman had made that opening to me, it chased me incessantly into my bride's proximity. I entered three or four times a day into the gothic house without having a reason for my appearance, and then listened furtively with pounding heart to the merchant's every word.

A not too numbing, inner voice muttered to me incessantly that he wanted to rob my warm, rosy treasure from me – that the heavy iron door of the patrician's house could still close in front of me before the end.

But nothing happened.

One day I heard in my study how Lilli in the next room asked my mother about the reason for my unrest.

"I can't see him suffering so," she said – "it seems then to me as if I myself suffer the most unbearable pains."

What a gentle, agreeable sympathy. How deep her affinity for me must be rooted. It trickled cosily through my veins.

And I heard my mother reply, "My daughter, the wedding is getting closer. That's probably why."

Then the two women whispered to each other.

I leant back in my chair.

Yes, the wedding was getting ever closer. The festive, mysterious moment would occur where to my mind two beings would merge bodily and spiritually in each other, mutually gifting their best.

And appallingly – while I was thinking that, a shiver ran through me. I knew exactly that Lilli was chatting in her yellowy grey autumn gown in the adjoining room. A reddish brown Rembrandt hat certainly wavered on her locks, her thin hands were presumably covered to the wrists with tight Danish gloves. – And yet – and yet – – then I dreamt of her again before me – the majestic divine figure, rosy and white, as she stretched out to me her dazzling arms, to me who remained consumed by desire and shaken by fear, firmly rooted before her.

My breath faltered.

Then the outer door opened.

Uncle Holm hobbled in, spat, and cried happily, "Boy, am I disturbing you? — My neighbour, Mrs Muchown, has slaughtered her pig, and I'm bringing you a piece of pork sausage. Exceptional — I tell you — exceptional."

I started.

The dream figure fluttered away.

***

The wedding was getting ever closer.

My students in the seminar smiled when I seemed distracted; Professor Wackermann squeezed my hand suggestively more often, and said once with a jovial flash of lightning in his friendly face,

> "it's one of the greatest gifts of heaven,
> such a dear thing on the arm to be havin'."

"Karl, Karl, now your most beautiful time is coming. Boy, how happy you must be."

Most obviously, however, Uncle Holm revelled in his earthy allusions.

"It must be a boy, Karl," he stipulated once very definitely, while he was eating lunch with us, "and then he can also be named after me — Jochen or Johann. As you like."

I do not know if such hints offended me in the slightest. I myself often felt ridiculous then, and even the woman who remained mine seemed to me degraded by it.

Only my mother seemed to comprehend the inner fear and shaking, my boundless uncertainty. When a load of new books arrived for me once, she was sitting, busy with her work, in my study.

I arranged the books on the shelves.

Then the little woman let her knitting fall, and sighed deeply.

"Boy, boy, haven't you been sitting too long with your books?"

"But mother, I've only been working a couple of hours."

My mother turned her head, and looked down at the river gliding past ponderously. "I don't mean today," she said finally in a low voice.

Then she quickly grasped her needles again, and let them clatter against each other.

My mother had vocalised what was pushing me about with dull suspicion.

Remaining too long behind the wall of my books, cordoned off too long from the fresh, rolling life that I did not know.

Whether that would never again be harvested?

A feverish greed took possession of me, in the short span which still remained to me, to make up for if possible what I had neglected up to then.

It is disgraceful to confess it. But I began to feel delight in all the recklessness of my students.

More and more, I felt ashamed of my own inexperience.

And then an incident happened in my life which swept away all these thoughts like the north wind which blows through the chaff, an experience which drove me away from the temple of ugliness on whose steps I lay already worshiping on my knees.

VII

Lilli and I were invited by the Rector of the university to a ball. I had never before seen my bride so beautiful, so glamorous and accomplished.

Even today the sea-green colour of her dress is memorable to me, even today I can see her proud, white neck shimmering out of it like glistening foam driven on the green sea, even today I can feel the glamour and brilliance of her blond hair.

Like an audience-giving princess, she stood out from the circle of her admirers.

I stood in the distance with the host, and observed her. From time to time, a gentle, gracious hand gesture, an ingratiating answer to something obliging that was said to her, a subtle turn of her pliant body.

And yet I felt distinctly that her look sought far over all the others to me and me alone.

Her blue eyes spoke quite clearly to me through the entire length of the hall, "Come, lead me away from this loud circle. I would like so much to be alone with you — all alone."

As though drawn by an irresistible current, I approached her. She withdrew from the others, and laid her arm in mine. I felt a strong, passionate pressure.

I could not even then see enough of this proud beauty.

We had soon said our farewells.

I myself girded her in the cloakroom in the protective shell, the long blue theatre coat with the white feather trim and an enchanting hood of the same colour.

Oh, how mischievously she sparkled from under the feathers. This flight from society seemed to provide her unending delight.

Down on the dark, deserted street, the old French carriage of the merchant was held ready. I lifted her in, sat down next to her, and barely had the wagon begun to roll on the cobblestones than Lilli had nestled on my chest, slung both her arms around my neck, and offered me her lips with such a devoted expression that I could have crowed out loud. Then she stammered something unintelligible; but straight after, as if she were ashamed of this outburst, she pulled away from me, though pressing her hand in mine tempestuously.

"Oh – you – you," she stammered.

"Now, what is it, child?"

"How wonderful your toast was before. That easy, delightful verse. I have never heard such a thing before. They were all completely taken, and I was generally congratulated."

"Oh, ridiculous –," I fended it off, flattered.

And yet her praise shook through me pleasantly, and made me bold.

It was so dark in the wagon. The town was sleeping. I embraced her; she smiled, and again our lips met until I could feel her small teeth.

Then she began quickly to continue chatting blissfully and excitedly, "In a few days, you will also be a Professor, the Rector told me."

"Yes, but I must still be confirmed."

"And your book about the folksongs is so brilliant."

"So, did he say that too?"

How this academic recognition did me good. As a result, I almost forgot that I was sitting next to a young, fervent woman.

She continued ever warmer and more impassioned, whilst pressing up to me trustingly. "But that is all the same," she whispered with a passionate voice.

"All the same? – Lilli –"

"Yes, yes, Karl – just think, in fourteen days, we have our wedding. Then I'll have you to myself, the famous husband. Oh, you don't know at all – As you stood before by the Rector with your fine, pale face, your dark, wavy hair and your large, brown eyes, you seemed to me so exceptional, so wonderful – you – you, I think I shouldn't tell you everything at all actually. Oh, just think, in fourteen days, we have our wedding."

And again I felt the gentle, devoted touch on my arm; the white feathers of her hood trembled against my temples, and I – what a miserable power was controlling me? – I sat there again as if I were a hundred miles from her – restrained, discouraged, and peered through the steamed up panes at the small, pointy gabled houses of the street. The moment which my bride yearned for rose up before me, warning, threatening, filling me with an inexplicable fear.

Then the carriage stopped.

A servant stood under the portal of the gothic house with a lantern.

We climbed out.

I did not know, to me this separation seemed almost like a deliverance, I had almost a desire to be alone with myself and my uneasy feeling.

Under the old, narrow-ribbed portal, my bride offered me her hand once more. I led her fingers to my mouth while I noticed what a full, devoted look she gave me.

The lantern threw wondrous shadows sometimes on Lilli's face, sometimes on the ancient pointed arch of the entrance.

At this moment shortly before parting, I suddenly felt again the old, wild tenderness flaming up in me. Yet a short, ardent whispering, then the heavy oak door was moving on its hinges, and I stood alone in the night of the market.

I ambled back slowly.

Behind me, I heard the dull rolling of the carriage driving into the gateway.

Then everything was still.

The small town was sleeping.

The lanterns had been completely extinguished, the houses abided in deep blackness. Nowhere a light, nowhere a sound, only on the corners did you hear the sharp wind off the sea.

Thus I strode along the narrow lanes with the low houses, and listened to the echo of my own steps.

And again tallied all my thoughts on the woman whom I had just left.

Was it not strange that I was always consumed with desire for her as soon as I dwelt distantly from her?

Further and further, I wandered down the street which led to the harbour; already the swishing and squalling of the wind howling out over the open countryside was lashing at my ears; then – I hesitated – from a slanting, single storied house, loud song was ringing out. A harmonica was adding its long drawn out tones in between, and the trembling sounds of a guitar were mixed into it.

When I stepped back onto the roadway, I read under an old lantern swaying back and forth creaking on an iron hook over the door the name of the premises.

It was a mariners' hostel, and it was called "The Green Herring".

The singing became louder, women's voices joined in.

A strange desire crept up on me to listen to the melodies of the folk up close for once. For many years, I had engaged myself with collecting every possible forgotten song, and here, here the folksong bubbled up perhaps fresher and more genuinely that I had ever conceived. What did I really know of the lower classes of the community in whose midst I lived? Had I not always wished to fathom life in its depths?

I made a sudden decision, and opened without further consideration the humble, green-curtained glass door which led into the premises.

A bell set off by the door rang out, but I myself saw nothing at first.

Thick, bluish grey tobacco smoke surged heavily back and forth in the narrow space, an unbearable heat reigned, and a strong smell of evaporated spirits and wet clothes struck me.

On my entering, the singing and laughter had stopped, but now rough laughter was rising from the men's throats and, at the same time, I felt myself being grasped by the hand by soft fingers.

A young whore with shaggy brown hair and large, sparkling eyes drew me fully into the room, and before I could recover properly from my surprise, I was sitting at a small circular oak table.

Now I could also gradually discern my immediate surroundings.

Five men in thick blue seaman's overalls were sitting around a longer adjoining table. They had their elbows propped on the table, before them stood schnaps and beer glasses; three of the young fellows each had a young female next to them, similar to the one who had drawn me into this circle. She herself, however, crouched at my table over by the end of their table, and began just then to play a new song on her guitar. The younger party started bellowing while a fat, bloated mariner held his arm around the hips of the singer.

An old pendant lamp spread some light blearily through all the blue fumes. The inordinately stout landlord leant behind his counter by the bottle shelf, and attempted to accompany the guitarist on his harmonica.

"Bum – dideldum – hopsassa" screeched around me.

A hefty distaste rose up in me.

So that was the song of the folk? And those young whores with the very low cut blouses, they were the creatures to whom these crude fellows brought their love? Oh, how fortunate I was that I lived in a protected world, how pure, how untainted the picture of my Lilli rose up before me. By God – was it not sinful, deeply despicable, that I had yearned even a short while ago for all these ugly things which were playing out at the moment so coarsely before me?

Louder and louder the music swirled, two of the couples began to dance with each other, and every movement which thereby surpassed the proper measure was praised by the fat landlord with raucous laughter.

"On and on —" he shouted, "so it's good."

It finally occurred to me, as if the rabble was exposing all its vulgarity so nakedly before me just to slight me, the better dressed one.

Ever stronger and more urgently, I had to think of Lilli. Oh, I was fortunate to call the purest, the most virginal woman my own. And here, here in the midst of all the hideousness, I shared for the first time the same hefty desire of my bride for a quicker union, to hesitate not a day longer.

Yes, yes, now she had to become mine, I did not want this precious purity to be separated from me any longer.

Quite suddenly, I realised what a blessedness awaited me.

***

Ha, ha, whilst I was writing this, I heard next to me the wild laughter of the lunatics raving in their cells. It sounded like an answer to my childish delusion.

Ha, ha, blessedness in rosy red clouds.

The lunatics are laughing again.

***

But at the time in the hostel "The Green Herring", everything in me thirsted for this glorious untouched state.

It seemed so hot. I had unbuttoned my coat; as a result, my tail coat became visible.

When the rabble noticed the festive dress, they whispered amongst each other. Then the guitarist sprung towards me, and sat down directly before me on the surface of the table. She then let her slender, black stocking covered feet dangle back and forth gracefully. I noted that this painted lady had in mind some sort of impudent intimacy, I saw how she slowly and smiling bent down to me, then – then – my entire life spent up to then in the quiet scholarly room rebelled against such a fall. The distaste shattered over me. I sprang up, threw a coin on the table, and plunged out onto the street amidst the mocking laughter of the drunken sailors.

"Bum – dideldum – hopsassa" it squealed behind me.

A few dark heads clustered in the doorframe to gaze after me, but I sucked in the fresh air outside, and ran, almost as if I were being chased, towards our little mariner's home.

"Thank God!" I was still thinking, while I climbed up the narrow, well-trodden wooden steps, "thank God that the muck never touched you, and that you will now be forever going towards purity."

VIII

Thus the last day had arrived. The last day on which I was alone.

"So no stag do?" regretted Uncle Holm, who hobbled in to my room in the early morning, and shook his grey head disapprovingly. “Why actually not, Karl? You would’ve laughed over mine. I wanted to come to such a thing as cupid, if needed even in a skirt; quite short.”

“Yes, uncle,” I responded, busy at my desk – “my father-in-law ordained otherwise. Tomorrow on the other hand is the great wedding.”

“Agreed, I’m even invited.”

“Well, obviously.”

“Tell me one thing, boy, do I also get a dinner partner? I’m not really properly familiar anymore with any fine wenches.”

“Eh, uncle, a man of your experience – –”

“Yes, Karl, you’re right, always valiantly working away. And finally, if you let the females eat in peace, then they do nothing for one either. Well? Isn’t that right? Now, tell me please, and after the wedding?”

“Then we’re going to Rügen.”

“Thunder and lightning – then it’s right. Up there on the island, there’s such a good, choice little hiding place. Quite for the honeymoon. Karl, my boy” – here the old mariner limped over to me, and clenched me powerfully in his arms. “I have my joy in you. Now you will also become something. Pay attention! And your little thing of a bride, that is a capital wench, a textbook example. Loves you also quite atrociously, that you can bank on, for I can read people. But now it comes to the crunch, now you must also know how to handle her.”

“What do you mean, uncle?” I asked more attentively while I bound together a bundle of colleagues’ books.

The Captain straddled a chair, and pawed with his feet.

"Well, you must wear the trousers, Karl; women with trousers, that is rotten. And with you book owls, that is what it mostly comes to. When your woman first knows that you have no idea what your own coat costs, then she will laugh secretly over you, and when the women first laugh over you, then a bit of love always swims away with it."

"Do you really mean that?" I stuttered, nervously tying up the bands of my books. My heart was hammering all the way to my throat. "Do you really hold me to be completely impractical, uncle? — Then it would be really — actually presumptuous — that I and Lilli — —"

My trembling voice must have made a strong impression on the old man, for he suddenly clasped my knees in his seated position, and roared good-naturedly, with the corners of his mouth twitching, "Eh, nonsense, boy, look, here in your learned hocus-pocus, you are a quite magnificent man in whom everyone must delight. And now — and now — — tell me one thing —" the old mariner wanted by all means to change the subject — "tell me one thing, what actually are you knotting together?"

With that, he pointed at my books.

"Oh, that concerns my work, uncle. I am taking it with me to Rügen," I answered dreamily.

"To Rügen?" Uncle Holm rose laboriously, spat heftily, and laid his fist heavily on my shoulder.

"No, boy" — he murmured with penetrating power, "don't do that."

I stared at him. "Why not?" I asked blankly.

The old man became angry. "Leave the stuff at home," he shouted. "Do you understand me?"

He slammed his fist on the desk, and pushed my papers to the side.

"Uncle!" I erupted fiercely. It shot through my head how much effort I had put into these notes, and what pure joy I, as well as Professor Wackermann, experienced in their discovery.

"Leave the stuff at home, Karl," the old Captain insisted, and looked me in the face with his bushy browed, glaring eyes so dominant and experienced in life that I fell silent before them. "Follow my advice, my son. You should read from a beautiful book up there. Understand, from a human book. There is much in them that you do not know. Believe me. And anyone who gets that book in the hand as beautifully white and pure as you, he should thank God, and not think at all at first of such stuff as that on the desk. Well? Right, don't you think?"

He brushed his calloused hand slowly over my cheek, put his cap on, squeezed my hand, and shuffled whistling out of my room.

I stared after him.

***

In the afternoon, I saw how my mother was packing a suitcase for me.

Over the last period, the little woman had gone about almost always close-mouthed, almost soundlessly. Only sometimes, when I was working, did I occasionally feel her gentle fingers caressing my hair. She did not speak, but her glance embraced me with a tenderness as though the minor journey to the island could decide between life and death.

The poor, old woman. How I will love her to the grave.

I myself remained calm. The inner agitation had in the last days reached such a degree that I became outwardly indifferent.

In the afternoon, my mother brushed my wedding suit and carefully laid a white cravat on it. She handled everything with a touching, delicate festiveness. She even stuck a cross shaped bone secretly into the pocket. She had kept it for me for a long time, it was meant to bring me luck.

I stood in the twilight hour at the window, and looked down at the dark river.

In the red of evening, I saw gleaming water lilies, and colourful tar spots swimming, I looked a long distance over the stubble fields to the church towers of the nearby fishing villages at the river mouth, always calm and motionless, as if I were not standing at the turn of my fate.

This absolute indifference which hindered me from thinking of the most obvious thing, of my beautiful woman, is still incomprehensible to me today.

Only once did my mother stroke my arm fondly, and ask, "Now, boy, you won't be anxious surely for me?"

And I replied quickly, "But, mother, how can you ask that? Just think, Lilli has promised to write to you straightaway on the first day."

"What? Has she – promised that?" the little woman murmured quietly; then she scurried back again to my suitcase.

***

Towards evening, I visited my bride.

I found her in a wide, half-darkened room on whose walls there were many tall oak cupboards.

Across a chair, a silk dress shimmered in bluish white, a pair of delicate white shoes standing before it. For a moment, Lilli remained motionless in the middle of the room, then she stepped quickly over to me, led me soundlessly to the window, slung her arm around my shoulder there, and leant her head gently against my chest.

All without a sound breaking the twilight stillness.

Silently, and yet bound intimately to one another, we both stood and looked lost in thought at the solitary dark chestnut tree in the courtyard, in whose branches the blue evening mist was already weaving.

From St Nicholas's church nearby, the evening bells rang out.

She shivered, struck by the ringing, and looked fully up at me with her dark eyes.

I drew her tighter to me. All without a single word. That soundless being together, that perfectly happy indifference to the world during that evening actually forms my happiest memory.

A dove whirred from its nearby perch past the window. It startled both of us. Once more I stroked her hair gently, she lifted her mouth towards me, and kissed me.

"So, till morning, Lilli," I whispered softly.

She squeezed my hand strongly, and nodded gently. Then I had the door in my hand, and saw the slender girl still turned away dreaming in the twilight.

***

Someone wants to take my book from me.

My treasure.

Professor Wächter has charged my warder with finding out what I am working on.

The rough, uneducated man. Always when I am seemingly not paying attention to him, he leans over the desk drawer, and rummages about in it with his calloused hands.

Oh, how I secretly giggle about him.

"You will not discover my treasure, simple-minded proletarian – you are not the man to outwit Professor Barkentin; – yes, if you slashed my night pillows, then perhaps – – But then – I would smile at you, inept fool!"

IX

The organ droning – the singing of children's voices – and the loud reverberation of the clergyman's words.

With a strange resoluteness, I saw and heard everything.

She stood next to me on the steps of the altar.

She had placed her slender, full arm, tightly encased in the heavy silk, softly under my own – it filled me with no excitement at all. – The bride's veil flowed over her lowered head, and trembled up and down imperceptibly with her breath, and I followed this tiny motion with extreme attentiveness; I did not know it was as if I were taking the greatest care to let myself be distracted by all sorts of trifles, only to not listen to the white-haired, small Pastor whose words my bride, like the entire congregation, seemed to be deeply seized by.

It sounded so strange, I was frightened before the solemnity of the moment.

Behind me, I heard sobbing.

It was my mother, who was sitting in the first pew next to Lilli's father. I heard distinctly how the merchant whispered to her in his superior voice that she must calm down. Then there were a few hefty snorts. That was Uncle Holm whose emotion expressed itself more energetically.

The clergyman spoke ever more animatedly and insistently, he was now directing his words at me.

"Go, my son, now you have won a virtuous woman, and keep the fire of your hearth in a pure blaze, for the purpose of the husband is to govern and to guard, and the fate of the wife is to love and to endure."

The organ, men's and children's voices thundered powerfully as one up in the choir, Lilli shivered, and I felt how her limbs shook.

The ceremony of the exchange of rings was approaching.

A whisper went through the wedding party.

Then my glance, which was straying about in erratically in the front of the nave, fell sideways as though in flight on a group of men whom I only knew variously as my father-in-law's captains. Right in front by a column, exceeding the others in stature and breadth, stood a still-young, sandy-haired, freckled skipper with long arms. He wore the becoming full dress uniform of a commander of a large passenger ship; he kept his red bushy-browed eyes fixed on my young woman, and in the motionlessness of his strict, energetic face, I noticed the almost captivating effect that my bride must bring out in others.

That suddenly returned me to life.

My heart began abruptly beating loudly before her beauty, I felt that I was certainly not worthy of so much glory. But no, when she noticed my movement, her eyes met only mine. With unending, yearning devotion, she turned to me so that I now lost all composure.

Oh, how tender and blissful the myrtle wreath's green was on her head.

No, no, all thought of this pure woman belonged to me, to me, the fortunate one.

Everything further elapsed as though in a half fearfully, half happily spinning dream. We exchanged rings. She pulled back her veil a little at the same time, and looked at me. It seemed to me as if an angel were standing opposite me with a message of hope. And yet I trembled at this moment from head to foot. Then we strode out, the full tones of the organ following us to the portal. Before us walked two little girls strewing flowers before our feet. And outside, the sparkling and radiant bride's carriage was already waiting.

And among all the pious tones, I suddenly heard the voice of Uncle Holm, who was following us with my mother on his arm. "Be quiet, Marie, but dammit, it was really quite solemn."

I lifted my bride into the white silk cushions of the carriage; as I shut the door behind me, I was overcome with nervousness by the feeling that I was also closing with a bang at the same time the gate which would separate my life up to then from my new one.

My bride sat with lowered head. Her breath was short and gentle.

***

Only the shadow images scurrying past, barely comparable to rushing dreams, have remained with me from the actual wedding reception. All is unclear and indistinct. In the great hall of the lodge house, we sat at a horseshoe shaped table.

Many radiant merchants' wives, many officers with sparkling uniforms, opposite me a whole row of venerable university heads, among them Professor Wackermann grinning proudly behind his blue glasses from time to time at my bride as if he wanted to call out, "You can talk of happiness now you've received it."

The table was decorated with flowers. Lilli and I sat behind a massive, ten-armed silver candelabra whose candles radiated brightly.

I do not know if I felt how we became more and more self-conscious before one another, how I chattered with her absentmindedly, and how she also lost much of her certainty. Under the trembling shimmer of candlelight, her colours, when I responded to her, would often shift from glowing red to the snowiest white.

Oh, in her confusion, in her weakness which confused me as well, lay such a dangerous charm. I caught myself staring at her sometimes as if she were a charming wonder completely unfamiliar to me.

And then what I today like to call the "reminder", the "warning", began to penetrate into my wedding.

Professor Wackermann tapped on his glass, and made a toast. It began at first very jovially, and was aimed directly at Lilli.

He had to share with the young lady something unpleasant. Her husband would not in fact be an easy gentleman to look after.

They laughed over this beginning, they waved to each other, Lilli squeezed my hand under the table, only my mother looked over offended at the speaker.

Yes, the Professor continued while he held one hand under his old French tail coat, and pointed with the other at me, Doctor Barkentin has a good fairy. That is his scholarship, the legend, the folk tale. Meanwhile, the young wife would not like to undervalue this love. For over many years, the folk tale has reigned in the cosy mariner and scholar's house, the couple – the quiet academic and the spirit child – will have looked with clear eyes deep into one another to the depths of the soul.

Now the living, the blossoming, the young wife sits by the scholar at his desk, and here he, he, the awkward, old, dry Professor Wackermann, wants to give the beautiful young girl a reminder, a request on the way.

The Professor leant far over the table, and now talked to Lilli with deep seriousness, "You must step fully into our interests, my child," he concluded with soft, excited voice, "you must ungrudgingly leave the magnificence and brilliance of the great world behind you, and step with soft feet into the silence of our academic community, you must henceforth let the imperceptible joys of knowledge suffice, yes, you must yourself become like the quiet, clear folk tale, so that your Karl, when he turns around, thinks to recognise in you his old companion. But then, then, my child, your happiness will also ring out like a chime in the wind. Endlessly tender – endlessly harmonious!" – When the old academic had thus spoken, he sat down suddenly in his place without having proposed a further toast.

Deep silence reigned in the hall.

To myself, it seemed as if a supernatural hand had unexpectedly torn a blindfold from my eyes to have me look into an endless, garishly grey distance.

Heftily, jerking, I turned to Lilli who had huddled up to me gently.

"Tell me," she whispered in a low voice, while her large eyes hung fearfully searching on mine, "will I even be able to fulfil all that which your friend desires of me? But, is it right, Karl, I will learn to, won't I, quite certainly, because I'm so fond of you?"

Her voice was trembling.

I looked at her.

Then the words of my warning friend were as though wiped away, I saw only how she changed colour, ashamed under my uncertain look. All reminder was forgotten.

She peered furtively under her dark eyelashes at the large clock up on the balustrade which ran around the entire hall.

The hand pointed to the sixth hour.

At ten o'clock, the train would snatch us to Stralsund. Our eyes met. A quite foreign, dancing world opened up before me.

I was not scared anymore, I was afraid no more, all my feeling had perished completely before the grandness of the new which was assailing me.

I still recall only two things.

Uncle Holm rose, and drank to the health of the Karström's house. "Since our Karl no longer has a dear father, and I am now probably actually the head of the family."

With the recollection of my father, I started, instinctively I had to look at my father-in-law. Was he likewise recalling that nasty conversation between us? But the merchant remained, as always, in his impenetrable calm.

And then the captains of the shipping line rose one after the other to give a quick cheer for my bride in the name of their ships and crews. As the last, that blond, tall mariner who had already attracted my attention fleetingly in the church spoke.

Am I seeking to convince myself after the fact? I do not know. – I have thought it over too much already, but it seems to me as if I had already at the time been pursuing with strange, fearful tension every movement of this tall, steely body. His energetic, bright eyes encompassed my wife with such a reckless tenacity, he raised his glass so markedly towards her alone as if he felt quite alone in the large party, as if he had a right to stare at her until I had to look instinctively at Lilli too.

"In the name of the crew of the ship 'Pride of Pomerania'!" he called loudly through the hall with a deep, pithy voice.

Something so young and powerful lived in that organ.

"Do you – know the – gentleman?" I asked falteringly.

Lilli was so calm. Innocently she shrugged her shoulders.

"Who is that, father?" she turned whispering to the merchant sitting next to her.

And then I heard the name for the first time.

"Captain Jensen – engaged him just a few weeks ago from Hamburg. Should be a very capable officer. Tomorrow he goes with the 'Pride of Pomerania' to South America."

Lilli repeated all this detail with her dear voice.

Thus I heard the name for the first time.

***

– – – – – Calm – calm – don't let the blood boil up again in the throat – don't stab at his name on the paper with the knife! Quiet, it is all over and – avenged.

But at the time, I was hearing his name for the first time.

***

I hear the train's wheels rolling.

On the red velvet cushions of a first class compartment, Lilli and I sit alone.

Outside on the heath of the moor, there is deep darkness. Only sometimes do the flickering lights of a settlement appear, inside the compartment is a cosy light. Opposite us, a sharply bevelled mirror reflects the flickering light.

She was sitting by my side in her dark travel dress. She had turned her head to the darkness, but her hand rested firmly in mine.

We both thought of the same thing, of the town drawing ever closer.

Muffled, half murmuring, we spoke about all sorts of things. About the wedding party, about the places we wanted to visit on the island.

Then she turned her beautiful countenance to me.

"Will we stay at Cona for a longer time?" she asked suddenly, leaning back to me.

So much humility lay in this question. It gave me a peculiar shiver that this proud creature wanted to make herself so dependent on me.

"If you wish," I replied with forced, cautious tenderness.

"Me? No Karl, only what you want."

Oh, her words sounded so warm. They drew me to her. Our heads bent down. Our lips found each other in a long kiss; breathing, we embraced each other. And the wheels rattled unchangingly, and outside the Pomeranian countryside drifted past.

The town moved ever nearer.

BOOK TWO

I

Cona! How a thousand mobile lights sparkle on the calm surface of the water. How the coloured points spring up ceaselessly into the radiant brightness. – Red – green – yellow.

The sea forms droplets in the sun.

It is as if a gently humming, shimmering fluidity is foaming in the wide basin. Agreeable, dreamy calm weaves across the narrow bay. Light smoke curls from the chimneys of the few fishing cottages which sink completely behind green orchards.

And at the back of the settlement loom the high, white chalk cliffs, and high above on their peaks, sombre, green fir forests stare blackly, threatening, taciturnly up into the air.

That is Cona.

The place where the fool's game of my life misled me with a few wonderfully charming scenes, the place where I, serious professional man, behaved like an amorous shepherd, the place where I first offended and egged on to later revenge the strange being that I had chained to myself.

Oh, I can still see myself. In a bright summer suit – for the days which the parting autumn gifted us were blessed — and with the straw hat, about which my wife had wound a colourful ribbon. In yellow leather shoes, I ran over the loose sand of the beach to spy out after Lilli.

I had left her for only a few minutes to ask in our fishing cottage whether the postman had brought messages for us; now I was happily holding a few letters from home in my hands. "Lilli!" I called loudly, for the wide beach was deserted.

We and a taciturn government assessor from Stettin formed the only summer visitors to the abandoned place.

I found the sought-after woman sitting on a giant, moss-covered beach boulder which lay hard by the sea and around which finely rippled wavelets were softly washing. I paused, and instinctively pushed at the golden pince nez which Lilli as bride had already gifted me as a replacement for my glasses.

In her bright silk blouse with the black mariner's knots, the short, dark little skirt, the yellow boots, and the straw hat on her blond hair, she made such a fresh, life affirming impression that I, mad fool, paused for a moment, as though entranced, to be able to admire with effort this enchanting creature who laughed at me so tenderly.

— Over the eight days we had dwelt in Cona, I had already observed her thus countless times. Each time something new occurred to me about her which enchanted me, for my eyes had changed, I was seeing everything in a different light.

Oh, I was sunnily happy, I, the infatuated, no, that is not the right word, I was floundering in a distant wonderland, I did not feel ground under my feet anymore, I did not know whether I was floating or walking; everything in me and around me had become new to me and yet more blessed. The entire roaring intoxication of possession flickered in me and rocked me as though in lovely forgetfulness.

She was for me the first, the only one, the most glorious of women.

She had woken me first to the joys of existence. And I, unworldly man of books, could not do enough with the new gift.

With her, the world, the creation, began for me.

Oh, how I smile now when I think of how I felt a sort of fear before this devoted being. For I saw of course that she also lived in the same intoxicated state as myself. She even seemed a different person. — Softer, gentler.

Yes, the days which the parting autumn gifted us were blessed.

***

The patients are being called for a walk. I will write more in the afternoon.

***

She was sitting on the massive, jagged beach boulder, and playing with her red parasol.

"Lilli — how did you get up there then? You are surely wanting to bar me? — Tell me?"

"If you leave me alone for so long," she pouted. And yet she darted a glance at me under her half-lowered eyelashes, which let me recognise distinctly her entire intent.

At the time, it enthralled me!

"I only fetched our letters — look, three of them. — Still unopened as yet — I ran myself quite out of breath to be able quickly to be with you again."

"Really?"

She nodded to me vivaciously, and then moved to the side on her boulder as if she wanted to make room for me.

A little board lay on the beach, which I shoved up against the stone, sprang up, and was soon sitting next to her.

She framed my face with both hands, and kissed me ardently and stormily. "You lover, – lover," she whispered hastily, then looked around abruptly. "Can anyone see us?" she asked blushing.

"Eh, no, child. The assessor has gone swimming. And afterwards, he'll sleep."

"So – then we are entirely alone. – You and I –" she said, "that is the most beautiful thing."

"Yes, the most beautiful of all."

We fell silent for a while as though lost in dream. The sea lapped gently on our stone. Lilli looked at me. Then I fetched the letters out of my side pocket.

"There is also one for you here, Lilli. From your father. Look what's on it: Mrs Barkentin."

But she shoved my hand with the letter away as if she did not want to know anything about it. Then she leant her head on my chest, and looked up at me with her blue eyes.

"What then, child?"

With gentle pressure, she drew me down to her, and again I felt the warmth of this lovely mouth until that indescribable, quiet, trembling joy overcame me anew.

When I straightened up gently from her embrace, I had forgotten my letters. Strange! In these eight days, almost everything which lay behind me had absolutely vanished. My entire life up to then seemed covered in a haze; only my young, love offering wife became ever more distinct to me.

We sat for a period nestled closely next to one another, and looked out over the wide sea.

A tepid breeze was slowly driving blue and green shadows over the surface. And far beyond towards the horizon, two tiny white sails stood unmoving.

You could have thought they were seagulls flying for the coast.

Quite far off to the side, as though in blurred clouds, I could discern the tip of a church tower.

"There lies our home town, Lilli," I finally began.

She shivered. Then she embraced my arm heftily. "Karl, you shouldn't look over there. Do you hear?"

A quite distant tone of fear was in her voice.

For a moment – I recall – I was concerned, but then I stroked her blond hair, smiling happily.

How proudly her countenance lit up, how consumingly fond of me, she must have been.

"I am thinking of nothing but you," I comforted her, and laid my hand on her shoulder. "Only of you."

She sighed as though in a dream. Then she sent a sweeping glance over the sea, propped herself on her bent arm, and quickly drew the letters out of my pocket.

"So now may I read?"

And again she embraced me, and again she rested for a moment smiling on my arm.

Then we broke open our letters.

"My father says hello," Lilli informed me after she had flown over her letter fleetingly, "our residence is already furnished. And what does your mother write?"

"Here, yes – she is well. But worries a lot – – – God, the poor old woman. We must write to her again soon, you hear? – – She is already living on the upper floor – and yes – oh, think, mother writes, Uncle Holm – do you remember Uncle Holm? – well, Lilli? – Uncle Holm is at the hunting lodge in the afternoon, and hopes to meet us there. – You are willing though? It isn't unpleasant for you? Think, Uncle Holm would be so happy."

But she did not refuse.

Ingratiating as ever, she had understood immediately. Only we had to break off unfinished if we wanted to reach the old man in time. Lilli sprang onto the beach, and brushed her dress down.

"That beautiful walk through the thick, virgin forest –" she cried excitedly – "with you alone, Karl."

She seized me under the arm, and drew me away with her. We had to rent a boat for a certain stretch. In walking on, I fetched out the third, still unopened letter, and examined the inscription.

"Oh, from Professor –"

"From whom, Karl?"

"From my friend Wackermann. My God, what can he have?"

In that moment, the grey walls of the university emerged before me. A comfortable, furtive feeling crept up on me at the same time.

But my young, smiling wife tore the letter from my hand, leaving me dumbfounded. Then she pocketed it.

"Not before this evening," she cried, "today belongs to me alone, Karl. I want to see at once whom you have locked in your heart more, me or the old Professor?"

She huddled up even closer to me.

And I, the subjugated one, squeezed her full womanly arm, which was laid gently trembling in mine — and was happy.

II

We arrived almost breathless at the hunting lodge. The entire hike through the deep, dismally dark, virgin forest with its playful reflections of light, its fenced-in wildlife parks in which slender roe deer stepped up to the wooden lattice, coaxing and sniffing — this entire hike had been like a single, mad exuberance.

Sometimes I startled myself. — Amongst all this chasing around, snatching, cuddling, hiding, kissing, and ogling, a thought occurred to me lightning quick, vanishingly quick, from another world, from the world on the other side of the sea, from the calm of my previous existence — jerking upwards, bookcases appeared before me — the little room — the burning copper lamp. — But all that was now just like a fleeting, strange breaking wave in my brain, then I just needed to look at the pliant figure of my wife who was hiding behind an oak trunk in front of me; I just needed to see her short skirt flutter, and I flew into her arms with that loud laugh which I had taken as my own.

Further – further – – –.

We arrived breathless at the hunting lodge.

In the open courtyard of the castle, Uncle Holm immediately caught my eye.

With his legs apart, the old Captain was sitting under an ancient lime tree and, despite the warm weather, had steaming before him on the table a massive glass of grog from which he was slurping comfortably every now and then.

It was Lilli who called out to him first.

"Light of God – children, there you are," he swallowed, and limped over to us.

As he thus stood before us, awkwardly aired his blue cap, and stretched out to each of us one of his hulking hands, it seemed to me then as if he were seemingly bringing the air of our mariner's house with him. Certainly, I had never been so pleased by the old sea dog, and he also looked more and more delighted at Lilli and me.

"So – so," he nodded after the first greetings, laid his hand on my shoulder, and examined me in depth as if he were wanting to buy a horse. "Boy – how are you looking? – Red cheeks and tidy, a coloured ribbon around your hat? – Well, now look at this one, and tidy yellow boots? Now, how did you manage that, young woman?"

Lilli smiled.

Strange, for the first time, it occurred to me how in the presence of a third person, even in the presence of this harmless old man, she immediately became the distinguished, pale lady from the town, the patrician's daughter who only seemed to have entered our circle by a remarkable accident.

"You are very welcome, Uncle Holm," she spoke ingratiatingly while responding to the old man's handshake.

We took a seat at the table under the lime tree.

And the longer the mariner examined us, and the more I told him about Lilli and me, the more cheerful he became. In the end, he could not restrain himself anymore. "To your special welfare, young lady!" He wolfed down his glass of grog, immediately ordered a new one, and stroked Lilli's rosy little fingers lovingly with his broad, calloused hand.

"So no book has been opened? – Pert, what have I always said, something quite rational will be got from Karl. Don't you think, young woman?" He was stroking ever more intensively and strongly. Lilli's tender skin began to redden under his pressure. "But, six million score of herring, what sort of pretty fairy must you be too, that you manage such a thing? Well, for are you also fairly and truly fond of him, child? Well?"

My heart was pounding. How would she answer?

From Lilli's dark eyes flashed a ray of that restrained fire which was able to enliven this white countenance so remarkably. Instead of an answer, she just reached her hand to me across the table, but with such an unrestrained devotion that the old mariner lost himself completely.

I distinctly discerned how joy and emotion were battling in him.

He blew out a blast of air without, however, having a pipe in his mouth, slapped his knee, then shoved a new wad off tobacco between his teeth, and finally finished by whistling loudly for the waiter.

An adolescent boy rushed up breathlessly, and asked whether the gentleman wished for yet another glass of grog.

"Grog?" Uncle Holm growled, and took a look at the obliging boy, "no, my boy – – champagne – bring us a bottle of champagne – one of the finest – – Don't worry, Karl, I'll pay for it," he turned to reassure me.

And when the waiter left us, the old man moved closer to Lilli, and tapped her quite fondly on the arm.

I saw how a softly ironic look appeared around Lilli's fresh lips, and yet she did not seek to evade the Captain's caresses by any movement.

"So Karl has not opened any book?" Uncle Holm continued, humming softly. "And you have thus spent a proper honeymoon here? – Eh, I'll order a couple of dozen oysters with it; – doesn't bother me at all – Karl, my boy, it tickles me to do such a thing. Well? – Don't you think? –"

The champagne arrived.

Uncle Holm poured, and clinked glasses with Lilli. His grey eyes twinkled, his thick lips moved spasmodically as if he were planning something great; then he rose with propped fist a little over the table, looked blissfully around, and suddenly spoke a few awkward rhymes.

The unaccustomed wine had evidently gone to his head.

It sounded something like:

We sit under the lime tree
Quite close to the sea,
To your child, I drink the next round,
If I don't leave here beforehand.

"What do you think, Karl? That's by me. Made all by myself. – Cheers, young woman! Well, to the next year!"

How uneducated the old man behaved in every respect.

A distressing feeling crept up on me. How much Lilli's sensitivity must be injured. Only with effort did I venture to look into the countenance of my young wife.

And there – –

No, it must have been an illusion. At first it seemed quite incomprehensible to me. Around the young woman's fresh lips roamed a cheerful smile full of the freshness of life. She did not seem to take the tiniest umbrage at the Captain's rough utterances. On the contrary – they shook hands mutually, and let the glasses clink together once more.

A thought darkened me for the first time. "– – Look at her exactly; your wife is the fresh, free, natural life, she follows the general laws of nature – which you were alienated from for far too long by your imprisoned way of life. How would it be if you could now soon revert to that unhealthy shutting out?"

No, no, not brooding all the time!

I pulled myself together.

Around me wafted the fresh sea breeze, the massive lime tree rustled above me, and strew leaves down on us, and with me sat these two people who were so firmly rooted in life.

I sprang up, grasped my champagne flute, and cried out as though discouraged, "Cheers to life!"

"Our life, Karl," my wife whispered beaming. And Uncle Holm patted me on the back rowdily, and growled, "Karl – Karl – I rejoice over you."

III

It had turned towards the afternoon. The evening sun was falling reddish gold through the leaves. We had to take leave of Uncle Holm if we did not want to head home in complete darkness.

The wind was coming from the sea, and was already whistling coolly over us.

The old mariner had to inform me at the end of everything possible from home. In this way, I thought I had also detected that it was my mother who had directly prompted her brother to a journey to the island to ascertain how I was faring.

Oh, the dear, little, delicate woman with her overwhelming affection for me!

At the end, I inquired about my university friends, above all the Professor.

"Wackermann?" the Captain laughed as he accompanied us for a few steps, and rocked his head thoughtfully. "Well – he has recently brought you a quite magnificent wedding present."

And when Lilli inquired about it with interest, the mariner spat out his tobacco and, while he winked at me a little ironically, declared drily that it was an old carton. "Could also suggest pig leather. Well, in any case, something quite ragged and torn, Karl."

"Pig leather?" I repeated, taken aback. And suddenly I squeezed Lilli's hand jubilantly.

"For God's sake – just think, Lilli" – I cried out through the forest, "the Professor has brought us the monk's manuscript of Horace. – It is written in Low German. – The greatest treasure that he possesses – – the dear, old, discerning man. – No, how can I repay him for that? – Lilli, you aren't saying anything?"

"Me?" she stammered in bewilderment.

The Captain stared at me, dumbfounded. "Well then think on it," he growled. "I must return now. Adieu, children – adieu, dear young woman. – Do you know something new? If Karl had not married you already, and if I had been something fine, and if you had wanted to have me, then I would have married you myself – true, I, Johann Heinrich Holm. For you are a natural woman who fits into the world. – Well, and stay healthy now – Karl – and don't excite yourself too much over the gift of the mad Professor. – Adieu!"

He limped back.

We strode alone through the quickly darkening grove. We remained silent for a while. The red of evening was dying away. The wind was whistling ever colder through the branches. From the sea, we could hear a howling rising up.

I shivered, and felt comforted with the way Lilli nestled up to me. The warmth of this young body forced through me like a hot, comforting drink against the frost which was shaking all my limbs.

Ever anew, I sensed how beautiful she was.

It was getting darker.

Deep below us, the sea was rushing against the chalk cliffs. Massive blasts of wind chased through the creaking forest.

Instinctively, I slung my arm around Lilli, and she pressed herself trustingly against me.

“Are you freezing?” she asked me in the darkness. I denied it, whilst my teeth chattered.

Faster and faster, we ran through the steep forest.

“Oh – you dear, scatterbrained head, you,” Lilli suddenly giggled next to me.

I wanted to ask something, but the icy wind cut the words away from my mouth.

Then she pressed a piece of paper into my cold hand. Her fingers were still warm. Vivacious blood pulsed in them.

“Look – now you have forgotten your friend; here is his letter. – You were only thinking of me. Weren’t you?”

She suddenly threw her arms around my neck, and kissed me vivaciously. “Hey – how cold you are, Karl,” she cried with her fresh voice. “But now we will soon be in our little room. There I’ll get a little fire lit. Then it will be cosier, won’t it?”

And again she pressed herself against me, and pulled me onward.

I had clenched the Professor’s letter which I could not read because of the darkness and frost.

***

It was an hour later.

In our room’s squat, green tiled stove, a bright fire was flickering.

Outside, the sea was raging, the storm rattled the panes of the little Cona mariner's house, and occasionally even caused the light of the lamp to flare up.

I will never forget that evening.

Never.

Lilli undressed in the tiny adjoining room in which we slept, and got into her night dress.

I heard her rustling and chattering next door.

I pulled out by the low lamp the letter which I had not read.

My head glowed, whilst my feet were penetrated by an icy chill. My pulse hammered and shook, I felt that a fever was coming on.

That walk home with the icy northeaster had done it to me.

Nevertheless, I flew over the few lines breathlessly.

And then — —

"Lilli — Lilli —"

What was it?

My eyes glazed over. It seemed to me as if a thick, white veil were drawing through the room.

And yet it was there quite distinctly in Wackermann's enormous letters. — I had been made a Professor. — The new edition of folk songs had obtained me a chair.

"Lilli — Lilli!"

"Karl?"

"I've become — a Professor."

Next door, it fell silent. I spun around. I thought she would have been standing next to me long ago. This delay made me impatient.

The fever was already rolling in me.

"Why don't you come then?" I shouted.

Then she flew in to me.

Her night dress was still open, flying red ribbons fluttered behind her, a white strip of her skin which had to infatuate gleamed out, but I saw nothing – nothing of her beauty.

She kissed me, she caressed me, she gave me thousands of loving names, she bent over me finally, and cuddled my hands – in vain – I think I, fool, did not notice any of that at all. – I thought only of myself, and just stammered occasionally, "Professor!"

Then I bent down again over the letter. The fever was spraying from my eyes. Even Lilli noticed it.

"Come, Karl."

Her call sounded so anxious. My mother could not have asked more tenderly.

Oh, and I, fool, perceived nothing, I ignored the ardent love's lament which I later craved so often in vain, which I would a year later have wailed on my knees for, I rummaged through my letter like a mad man.

There it was.

"One is in general curious about your inaugural lecture. Have you diligently prepared? And could you perhaps find a few new folk songs over there?" – – – –

New – folk songs? I stared at my wife who had grasped my hand.

Outside a blast of wind cracked against the wooden walls so that the cottage seemed to lean over. The sea raged and roared its earth hungry song.

"Come, Karl, that's enough for today."

I looked around excitedly into the corners.

"What are you looking for?"

"My books –"

She took a step back.

If the fever had not already been racing loudly in my veins, I would then have noticed how a shiver flew over her glowing red cheeks.

"Your books?" she breathed.

Then I had already found behind the cupboard the bound-together pile. Impatiently I tore at the string, and spread the books, volumes, and maps on the table.

I only wanted to order, to seek out, to make myself a plan. In eight days, my lectures would already be beginning. And because of my wife, I had neglected until now all preparations. She could hardly be responsible for that.

How every line of my books shackled me, how every volume brought back a flood of memories.

While I was staring at the table, I sank into this world of notes as though into a soft bed, as though into a cosy bath.

Lilli leant on the doorpost of the adjoining room. She followed me wordlessly. Only her breath forced its way occasionally to my ear.

Then I turned impatiently to her. Her eyes embraced me.

"Go to bed, child — I will stay up a moment longer — a minute — I want to write up quite quickly the course of my lectures — I must now — I have neglected too much already — right now after my appointment — — —"

And again a new marginal note in my books seized me.

I saw and heard nothing more. Behind me, it went quiet. A sound still penetrated to me as though the door was being shut.

Undisturbed, thank God.

It roared and rushed in me. The cold cut through me so that I opened the door to the stove from time to time to hold my hands over the flames.

But the fever buoyed me.

I sat down, and began to write. When I rose, I staggered.

It was dawn. From the extinguished fire of the stove, the storm was driving out the last sparks — —

But I laughed: ha ha — I, the fortunate one — I had become a Professor.

IV

When I wanted to rise the next morning, I found myself seemingly crippled.

An appalling ache was eating at me brain, my tongue seemed to have stuck dry in my mouth, and my skin was burning me like liquid fire.

That was the aftereffect of the madly spent night.

Oh, and Lilli was leaning comfortingly over my bed, she brushed my hair wet with sweat so gently from my brow; she seemed to be deeply concerned over my illness.

"But it will certainly already be better tomorrow," she consoled me with her bright voice, which she could dampen down so soothingly, "such an attack of fever flies away so quickly, Karl. — By the way, I sent straightaway for the doctor. If he only weren't two hours away." — — —

A bleary period then followed, which still torments me in the remembering.

A creeping, ever returning fever had seized me. The country doctor's medicine proved powerless against it. But stronger still than the bodily heat was the torment of the intellectual fervour — the mad desire to work, the hefty longing to be able to operate in my profession.

My young wife had difficulty suffering with me.

Today I hardly comprehend her unending patience, her meekness, her quiet, calming temper. At the time, however, at the time, something else was engaging me, miserable man, incessantly.

All my thoughts rambled about my songs and fairy tales; even when I was shaken in bed by the nasty chill, my lips still murmured broken verses.

Then Lilli, sitting next to me bed, would grasp my hand, worried, then she would offer me the fever-stilling drink or lean her cheek on mine as if she could bring me relief with her fresh skin pulsing with life. God, when her skin rested so still and peaceful next to mine, when her dark eyes seemed to peer so large and questioning into mine, then it pinched me all of a sudden as if she were raising a silent reproach against me.

But she uttered nothing of that sort.

Even during the days of my illness, I would have been able to admire that consistent noblesse born to her, which had so attracted my attention at the beginning of our relationship. Constantly observant and ingratiating, she remained at my bed, she performed every reach of the hand with a grace that ennobled every movement. She fell silent when I wished for peace – she chattered when it was needed to cheer me up, and through all that, a tone of love trembled, at first strong and powerful, then more timidly, and more restrained.

But I, unfortunate man, overlooked all that, strangely. Only songs swirled through my head – songs and fairy tales. And gradually the madness also stirred in me, that the tender woman wanted to implant the same interest for this thing which inspired me. I still remember one morning.

Weak and battered, I rested on my pillows. The attack of fever had broken with the dawning of the day.

Outside before the closed window, thick, woolly, impenetrable mist was billowing; it had swallowed the sea for miles around, and now stood there immovable like a ghastly unyielding emptiness.

I turned my aching eyes to it.

The grey wasteland held me strangely fast.

After some time, I began, "Lilli."

"Yes, Karl."

"Pass me the volume there with the green spine, please."

"You want – you want to read now?"

"Yes – yes – something has occurred to me – you know, you must hear it" – – I leafed hastily back and forth – "about the mist too. It'll please you, Lilli. I transcribed it myself from an old folk song. Here –"

There stood the verse:

> They climbed onto land, the giants,
> And shrouded it in white mist.
> The town was lost, the tower was sunk,
> Only sometimes did bells whimper
> Out from the billowing depths

As if the deceased were calling there.

Once more, I repeated the verse, then I asked, “Strange? — Don’t you think, Lilli?”

She let her hands sink into her lap and looked silently out into the grey masses. Her slender, white profile seemed immobile. A seriousness never seen before also appeared to me in that countenance then.

Then I urged once more.

“Don’t you think, Lilli, it’s very beautiful?”

Impatiently I tossed in my pillows. Then she nodded earnestly as if she could only now disentangle herself from her own thoughts.

“Yes, Karl, it may be very beautiful,” she conceded hesitantly, “but forgive me, it strikes me as sad, makes me recall too much the — past.”

“Everything is transient,” I lectured her, and looked in my volume. I hardly thought anymore about what I was saying.

She fell silent. And I sank for quite some time so attentively into my own notes that I had almost forgotten the lovely creature next to me.

Suddenly though, I felt that her dark eyes must be resting fully and demandingly on my countenance. Like a compulsion, it ceased me until I had to likewise turn to her.

She had furtively grasped my hand, and never, never will I forget the sweet and yet so deeply serious expression which she placed in her few, simple words. “No — Karl — you must never say that to me ever again. Not everything is transient — not everything.”

Then she bent slowly down, and laid her head on my chest. And barely audible, she thereby repeated a few more times, “not everything” – as if she wanted to imprint these words indelibly fast.

Suddenly her body convulsed, I felt how she was violently suppressing a sob, and how she clung ever tighter to me so that I could not inspect her countenance.

So I lay there, fearful, daunted, and did not know that I, poor learned man, had pronounced judgment on us both with a phrase.

***

I was sitting again at my desk. The illness had gone away after a few days, and left only a great weakness and irritability behind.

And yet I sat joyfully sunken in my volumes.

Lilli reclined next to me on the sofa, and was eagerly reading the previously printed edition of my songs. She was now assiduously eager to penetrate into my subject as far as she was able. Often she asked me about this or that expression; occasionally I had to give her a brief explanation of a mythological figure unknown to her. Then our heads bent close together over the book, and while she squeezed my hand gently and gratefully, I sought to teach her with inner pride.

Oh, these hours made me so happy. Here my work, and there my wife who strove for such a close intellectual connection with me. I was also proud of my scholarship which could win such a power over this beautiful woman.

“Mrs Professor,” I teased her sometimes, looking up from my work.

Then she bent her white countenance gently smiling, and leant for a second warmly on my shoulder.

Always meditative. – Yes, my scholarship must have done it to her.

***

Outside the autumn wind was wafting.

The rain had stopped, now scurrying sunshine was flying across the yellow sand. Before our windows, the sparrows were twittering. Their lively bickering startled me.

Strange – my wife had let her book sink into her lap, and was looking out motionlessly at the laughing sea.

I touched her.

"How lonely it is here," she murmured involuntarily. Then she rose, and opened the window. You could hear the loud breaking of the waves on the beach, and the purring of the wind. In this moment, Lilli nodded amiably, and yet genteelly as ever to someone passing by.

"Who are you greeting, Lilli?" I inquired, taken aback.

She shrugged her shoulders. "The assessor," she replied without interest. And half to herself, she added, "Tomorrow he departs as well."

For a while, it remained quiet between the two of us.

The tall figure remained turned away from me at the window, and let her eyes rest on the wide surface of water.

But in me, the words she had spoken echoed with hurting sharpness. Was the stay with me alone already becoming painful for her? I thought to myself that we were actually on our honeymoon, even if the end was also resembling more and more a hard-working study trip.

For the first time, I engaged myself with her again. For her words seemed to hurt me.

"Lilli, are you bored here?"

But she did not turn, just kept looking calmly over the glittering water.

I stepped closer to her. "Are you pining for home?" I asked more urgently.

Slowly she turned to me, and nodded wordlessly.

"Lilli," I cried reproachfully and grievously.

Then she grasped my hand.

"Karl," she started falteringly and did not raise her eyes from the floor, "yes – I – pine for our own home life."

"And why, Lilli? – why? – Tell me the truth."

Oh, and she never lied. – Never – not once out of pity did she speak an untruth.

"Here it is – so cold – and comfortless," she stammered.

For a moment, I stood as though turned to stone. It seemed to me as if an abyss had opened between us, from which a cutting cry of pain was screaming. I closed my eyes. But then I rushed up to her, kissed her hands and arms stormily, and whispered almost pleadingly to the surprised woman, "Lilli, shall we leave tomorrow?"

"Tomorrow?"

A sunbeam lit up her countenance. Again she just nodded. But her full mouth smiled this time. And suddenly she threw herself into my arms, and under all my kisses, I heard how she heaved a gentle, aching sigh.

"Lilli?"

"Yes, Karl?"

"You don't have anything against me?"

"Why do you think that, dear? – Nothing. No, but at home, you will also be able to work undisturbed. Right?"

"Yes, yes, you're right there," I cried joyfully, "I'll pack my books immediately. We shall head home."

We made ourselves ready to depart.

The next day, we left the island where we had spent our honeymoon. The ship cut swishing through the plunging green waves, and churned towards our home and – our destiny.

V

What had become of the simple living room of Captain Barkentin's little wife?

A distinguished dining room done up in dark colours with portières made out of soft, turkish carpets. Even electric light had made its way into the old mariner's house, and now poured its flood of light out of an English copper corona over the massive table covered with a white silk tablecloth, around which we chatted cosily over coffee.

At five o'clock, my dear little mother had received us with fir garlands and welcome greetings – almost sobbing with joy and emotion – down by the front door, and now – an hour later – the circle of our acquaintances had gathered to congratulate me and Lilli on my appointment.

There they all sat – even today I can picture them – Lilli's father in his immaculate black frock coat and the grey silk cravat; next to him, my dear, old Professor Wackermann with his antiquated collar and his good rapturous countenance above it; he was straightaway engaged in enlightening the merchant in depth over the worth and significance of folk songs. – To my side, in her Sunday-best silk dress, my good mother, who did not want to let my hand out of her own – and at the end of the table, ogling eagerly a large plate full of cakes, Uncle Holm, who, from time to time, threw a side glance at my father-in-law to see if perhaps this millionaire he held in high regard noticed his little skirmishes with the baking.

Oh God, why did this familiar picture have to fade so soon from my life? Why?

Sometimes a raging desire for that repose grasps me.

I would like to break out from the walls of this mad house, strangle and trample down everything before me until I succeed in getting out, out to the small cemetery to scrape dead Lilli out of the earth.

Oh, merciful God, just once more, lead me back to this circle of dear faces – just once more, take from me the memory that all my happiness was extinguished by a stream of red blood. For just an hour, let me forget!

Oh, my God – – – –

***

We were still sitting at the coffee table.

The company had expanded meanwhile. The rector of the university, Professor Krusius, a significant jurist who had married a noble lady, had entered and introduced his wife to my Lilli. Usually the lady of the aristocracy tended in her social interaction to be very select. Her visit taught me thus that I had also climbed socially through my entry into the Karström family.

And strangely, here, in this lively circle, my young wife appeared transformed; her eyes received again their previous subjugating brilliance, her movements became freer and less measured, she again knew something pleasant to say to everyone.

Even a pair of my favourite students and seminar participants had turned up. And soon these young people formed a sort of serving guard for Lilli.

There was in particular a fraternity student – a Count Kottop – a tall blond youth with a dead straight parting, picky clothing, and a few scars on his face, who exerted himself superbly about the new Professor's wife.

He carried her cup after her when she rose, he presented the misplaced lace handkerchief to her with a deep bow, he pushed the chair towards her at the fitting moment when she wished to sit down.

I smiled. And Lilli also smiled as she occasionally , almost imperceptibly, threw one of her sparkling looks at me.

The mark of this secret understanding delighted me. Yes, my beautiful, glorious wife knew to separate the silent, inconspicuous scholar nevertheless and in spite of everything from such sparkling social butterflies; she felt admiration and awe of me as of my scholarship, and I was convinced that this was the most certain foundation for love. — — —

Ha, ha, she felt desire, burning, consuming desire — — — and I —. Oh, at the time, I was probably really delirious and mad.

***

I still remember that we scholars retired for a moment into my little study.

When I pulled back the new portière from the door, I stood once again as if blinded and turned to stone. Even the two other Professors, as well as the students, burst out into an exclamation of astonishment. Lilli's father had not kept his promise. His wealth had also forced itself here.

"Boy — boy," Wackermann showed his astonishment, and adjusted his blue glasses. "You know how it looks here? — Princely."

"Yes, work could be done here," the Rector also affirmed with an approving smile while he let himself glide into a dark brown leather armchair, "dear Barkentin, I see you can be congratulated in every way — really sincerely."

And I had to confess, at this moment I myself began to admire wealth and what it was capable of.

Yes, it was my old room, and yet select taste had now lent it a comfortable, cosy, dignified tone.

Instead of my worm-eaten bookshelves, heavy, dark oak bookcases stretched along the walls, the floor was laid with various colourful, oriental carpets, an old German carved mermaid light sent its beams from the ceiling down to the sated colours, and by the window hung with curtains stood a massive, green covered writing desk on which my dear old copper lamp hung resplendent, and underneath it lay my books.

But above the small chaise longue, opposite the entrance, the white busts of Homer, Shakespeare, Dante, and Goethe greeted me.

The white light flowed over everything.

"Yes, work could be done here," the Rector repeated while he stroked the brown leather of the armchair, eyeing it up, and then he added, "Have you determined your lectures already, dear Barkentin?"

And Professor Wackermann, who was still standing astonished under the carved mermaid light, tapped me suddenly affectionately on the shoulder, and opined jovially, "Well, Karl, what beautiful thing have you brought us from over there? Hey?"

To some extent embarrassed, I confessed that my harvest was a very tiny one. I had been on my honeymoon this time.

"Yes, yes, right," Wackermann murmured, rubbing his forehead with astonishment as if he only now remembered it, "honeymoon" – and then across the smooth countenance of the scholar spread that world-enraptured, wistful look which always set in when he lost himself in his pictures.

"Yes, truly, it is glorious, Karström's rosy daughter, Lilli, a charming creation," he murmured to himself.

"Aha, he is with his friend, Homer," the Rector smiled, and waved to me.

But Wackermann did not let himself be disturbed. Ever more enthused, the blue glasses stared up into the flood of light as if, there above in long processions, the world of the Greek singer was flickering past, and with outstretched hand, he declaimed unconcerned:

> Nobody blamed the Trojans and brightly
> arrayed Achaeans,
> That for such a woman, they held out so
> long in misery!
> Like an immortal God for sure, she was
> by renown!*

A murmur went through the little room.

Truly, the old scholar tore us all away with his unaffected admiration.

"Bravo, colleague," the Rector murmured as he rose.

And then the dignitary approached me with that suggestion which defined my entire existence from then on, which would turn to ashes my life's work.

In the university library, there was an old folio which originated from a Cistercian Abbey near the sea. Old, barely decipherable Low German and Latin songs and legends were contained in it.

"I've actually been envisaging you for that for a long time, dear colleague," Professor Krusius opined, and patted my hand benevolently. "For I believe, for a man like you who is himself half poet, this undertaking must possess something exceedingly enticing."

"Boy," Wackermann called in between, "what do you say? That is something for us."

Then my nemesis took me captive.

A new world of work emerged before me. I saw myself in this comfortable room sitting at my table; I saw myself comparing, discovering, researching; the

* Homer, *Iliad*, Bk 3, 156.

entire quiet delight in knowledge of my profession came over me.

I grasped both the Rector's hands, and thanked him, thanked him devotedly for the black gift which would plunge me and the woman who had just been praised so enthusiastically into the abyss.

"Tomorrow I will have the folio delivered to you," Professor Krusius concluded, satisfied.

"Yes, and I will turn up tomorrow afternoon just as punctually," Wackermann nodded eagerly. "I may of course, Karl? We will hopefully be undisturbed here, won't we, just among us, my son? Eh, it will be a delight, I tell you. You can count on me."

He patted me cheerfully on the back, and drew me to himself as if the foundation of my fortune had just been laid.

The poor old man, he did not know better.

Then the portière rustled, there was a heavy knocking on the door, and Uncle Holm's rough voice called through the crack in the door, "Karl, people are leaving, you must accompany them out."

We followed the call.

***

That same evening, I was standing in the little bedroom of my mother. I still wanted to wish the old woman a "good night".

Lilli had retired to our apartment down below already.

The little white-haired old woman was already clothed in her night cap, and now stood at the simple birch-wood table on which a night lamp was burning.

She grasped my hand affectionately.

"Has she been paying proper attention to you," she inquired forcefully.

"Lilli?"

"Yes, your wife, Karl. I mean, she knows that your health – understand me right – that your health must really be conserved?"

But to me, a reminder of my less robust body was unpleasant, even torturous, and so I staved off all further questions quickly and apprehensively.

"Certainly, mother, Lilli is good, as good as you could not at all imagine; excepting you, certainly the best woman in all the world. You will also become fond of her."

An anxious smile flew over the withered mouth of the little woman.

"If she makes you happy, then I will bless her," she murmured simply, "good night, my son."

"Good night, dear mother."

***

My wife was still awake.

I sat down by her on the bed, she propped her head on her hand, and looked up at me.

"Our home is beautiful, don't you think, Karl?" she whispered softly.

"Very beautiful, Lilli," I responded, and stroked her blond hair thoughtfully.

She huddled up closer to me. "And what are you thinking now?" she inquired.

Then I, fool, told her about the work which the Rector had held out the prospect of to me.

It could be the work of my life.

"Now, Lilli, I am completely happy, I have my scholarship and you."

"And – me," she repeated.
But I heard nothing.

VI

An entire span of time flies past me, grey and undecipherable.

Our life must almost have flowed noiselessly on, for no audible sound rings out in my memory. I lectured to my students at the university in the morning; in the afternoon, I had to make preparations for the next lecture; and in the evening, I sank affectionately into the massive folio, into that almost inextricable monk's script which waited for my interpreting mind.

Then the old German carved mermaid light expended its familiar shimmer from the ceiling of my room, the copper lamp beamed cosily on my writing desk, and next to me, almost buried under books, my dear old Professor Wackermann crouched, drumming carefully with his fingernails the measure of the verses which he saw written down by me in rough draft.

"Boy, boy," he sometimes cried enthusiastically, "this monastic man is just like a Low German Homer. And how you know to render it. Quite – excellent."

Sometimes we heard Lilli knocking timidly at the door. At Wackermann's "come in", the slender figure, which is rememberable to me in this period almost always in a simple black dress, stepped erect and lithely into the study.

She tended never to sit without asking ingratiatingly beforehand, “Is it permitted?”

Usually we both then quickly called our approval, and she settled down in the armchair close by the stove to listen for hours to our expositions, and the disputes which were tied up with some translation.

Frequently Wackermann also turned to her, stood up, pointed with his finger at a place in the manuscript, and began enthusiastically to recite. “Well, Mrs Barkentin, how does that sound?”

Then she smiled approvingly, a quiet, tender smile which had not wanted to leave this proud, white countenance for some time, and then sat again soundlessly and calmly in her place, only her gentle breaths betraying her presence.

We continued working.

***

Thus it passed into winter.

Outside the snow fell in great white flakes. Like an eternally mobile shroud, it gleamed before my windows.

A bright fire burned in the stove of the study, red embers shimmered, and I listened delightedly, sitting at my work table, to the crackling and bursting of the wood.

Thus I did not hear Lilli entering the room.

Only when she had set down a glass of strong wine next to me did I look up at her.

“You’re back already from the university,” she asked calmly as she stroked my cheek softly, almost maternally, “and haven’t sought me out at all yet, Karl?”

“Me?” I murmured, and smiled up into her beautiful white countenance. “You know, such a good thought came to me straightaway, and then I sat down probably immediately. You will forgive me, won’t you?”

She just nodded wordlessly. Then she settled down gently on the armrest of my chair.

“Why are you working alone today?” she asked.

“Because Professor Wackermann has a cold.”

Interested, she bent down to me now as if she wanted to read what I had written.

“May I stay with you?” she then asked, looking up from below.

“Certainly, my child, just sit yourself down.”

And so she reclined in her armchair again quietly.

Outside the snow was pecking against the window panes. I noticed how my wife followed me incessantly with her large eyes; but strangely, that was comfortable for me. Her calm, sympathetic presence did me good.

We thus spent certainly more than two hours. I only heard the crackling of the pen during this time, and the gentle movements of my wife.

Sighing, I finally straightened up.

“Have I disturbed you?” Lilli asked, remaining erect, almost motionless in her armchair.

When I fixed my eye on this quiet woman abiding in marmoreal ease, then I was overcome suddenly with compulsive force as if I had to say something loving to her.

Quickly I stood up, drew her up by the hands from the armchair, and led her to my desk.

"Look, Lilli," I said, "when you are here, then it seems to me sometimes as if something of your calm, mellow soul streams into my writing. Then it is to me as if this poetry were actually created by both of us. – Do you understand that? – In a sense our child, Lilli, our spiritual child."

She stood so attentively before me. Suddenly an abrupt glow ran into her cheeks. And she immediately huddled close to me as if she wanted to listen to the pounding of my heart. Her entire body was trembling.

***

One afternoon – it was almost dark, only the stove fire was jerkily illuminating my room – Uncle Holm limped into my room.

"Boy," he called, "first I have to shake the snow off me. What sort of pleasant weather is this! My fingers have really seized up!"

With that he shook the flakes from his fur jacket, just like a hairy monster climbing out of water.

"So," he then gasped, "now you are taking liberties, Karl!"

He shoved a heap of books from the chair quite recklessly, and settled himself down, puffing and blowing.

"Yes, what do I want, Karl?" he then rasped. "You don't know, but I'll tell you. So, do you want to relieve me of a lot of red wine which I have just bought at the port? You must let me earn a bit by it, understand?"

"Red wine?" I responded, reclining by the stove, a little confused. "Yes, uncle, if you think – – – but I don't actually have any real need for it."

"So," the mariner roared, and rocked his head critically, "no need? – What are you saying?! – Well, I always wanted to ask you, Karl, don't you keep company at all?"

I answered no. We had not yet thought of it.

"Not yet thought? Well, and your wife, she doesn't want to either?"

And again, I had to respond quite impatiently that I had not yet obtained Lilli's opinion over it either. But she did not particularly go without companionship in my opinion.

"Well, for my sake," the old man sniffed, rose, and struck both his fists loudly against his shoulders to warm himself. "So nothing will come from that business with the wine. But some utterly practical advice, your Uncle Holm may provide you with again, may he?"

"Certainly, uncle – – but – – –"

"Now please listen to me, Karl. You're locking her away too much with your books."

"My wife?" I started, "whom I leave completely to her own will?"

"No, Karl, I'm not saying that. You're just exerting such a silent pressure over her, do you understand me? It is as if a crab has married a stickleback – don't you think? – There the crab is stuck constantly down below in its muck, but the stickleback wants to have water and a swarm of other little fish, and sunshine too. And if it does not have that, then it perishes."

I stared at him. Despite the warmth of the stove, a shiver ran down my back.

"Uncle, you're not saying though ..."

"No, no, Karl, that is just a poetic comparison of mine. Sit down calmly to your books again. And I will stick the wine on your rich father-in-law. Adieu."

With that, he lifted his boots up, and scraped his way coughing out the door.

***

A few weeks passed.

"Do you want to accompany me?" Lilli inquired on a clear winter's day.

The sun was flashing through the frost patterns on the panes, and the snow on the rooves opposite sparkled in wonderful splendour.

Through the half open door, my wife peered in a little, and behind her stood my mother, who offered me a "good morning".

"Karl," the little woman reminded me, and opened the door a bit further, "just look at Lilli. This beautiful fur jacket and the little cap with it. Really, I am quite proud of her."

And in fact, it was a cheerful picture to see my beautiful wife showing off in her winter costume.

She inquired once more, "Will you accompany me, Karl?"

A hidden, gently trembling request lay in it, which she had usually never expressed before me and in the presence of my mother.

Meanwhile, a walk around the winterly market whilst the small town's military band played seemed to me like a sin against my yet to be deciphered folk songs.

Aggrieved and silent, I looked at my manuscript.

"Karl, don't you want to?" my mother urged.

Even her tone sounded anxious.

Then I subjugated myself. I wanted to make the sacrifice. Sighing, I placed the large blotting paper over the sheets.

Only, I would not succeed in departing, Lilli stopped me. With lowered head, she explained that she knew that an interruption of this sort was unwelcome to me, she did not want to take it on herself, and so she would walk alone.

She became somewhat more paler still when she said this, but her voice did not tremble.

"Karl," my mother cried, upset, "you will walk with her though?"

But my wife had already turned away, and hurriedly left our apartment as if she no longer wanted to hear the little woman's request.

You could hear the glass door outside falling shut.

"Karl – Karl, what are you doing!" my mother murmured. And then she shook her old head worriedly, and left me alone.

I stood for a moment appalled, apprehensive, and startled before my book. But then the fury which filled my soul over this entire period seized me anew.

The book must be finished, it must be the most splendid, the most spectacular of its sort.

Onward – onward.

I sat down, and wrote.

VII

And Lilli herself reinforced me in the ill-fated delusion of her insoluble attachment to me.

Certainly, this faithful, true, strong character was only to be unsettled and sent off the rails by an unfortunate like myself.

I hardly noticed that, while the monk's script throve impressively under my hands, she became more and more addicted to physical exercise.

One day, the merchant appeared at my place, and reported to me, in his manner which offered no room for disagreement, that he had gifted his daughter a riding horse. He would accommodate it in his own stalls.

"You have nothing against that, dear son?" he added out of politeness.

I thought to myself, and shook my head. No, I would not begrudge Lilli any pleasure from the heart.

How gloriously she must have appeared on the horse! Then the people would have stopped and, at the sight of the lithe rider, whispered, "That is the wife of Professor Barkentin."

This picture did me good, it appealed to my poetic feeling.

And so my wife began to live outside the house more often than before.

I can still see her as she appeared one evening in my work room in a wonderful pink-coloured attire with long white gloves.

We were invited to a small party in the house of my father-in-law. I had already asked Lilli though beforehand to appear first in this circle alone. I intended to fetch her after several hours. For since the illness of my dear Professor Wackermann, it was absolutely necessary that I doubled my efforts on the work.

***

Oh, you miserable dead pages, you are marmoreal gravestones under which my happiness and my dead wife are now slumbering.

Sometimes it is to me as if I should cry out, “I curse you, fruitless scholarship that betrayed me! I mock you, you arid guild work which you buried for the earthworms and, at the same time, cut the scented flowers down to their roots!”

But then the horrific thought seizes me that I was perhaps a false priest of the scholarship. And then I sit huddled up in my cell, and – fall silent.

Silent, a buried man.

***

Barely an hour had passed since Lilli’s departure.

Then I suddenly heard quick steps approaching my room. The door was opened forcefully, and my wife in her pink silk dress stood before me.

Her cheeks were glowing, her golden hair seemed disarranged.

It even attracted my attention.

“Lilli,” I cried, “you aren’t ill?”

She brushed her forehead once quickly as if she wanted to wipe away a tormenting thought. Then she stepped up to me still more forcefully, and slung both her arms around my neck. Stormily she kissed me like she had not for a long time in those past weeks.

At the same time, I felt how her skin was burning.

"What's the matter with you, Lilli?" I urged with trembling voice, for I perceived that she must have been completely put out by something.

Then came the revelation.

She had sat down on the chaise longue, and was now uneasily stroking her silk dress. The material crackled and rustled under her hand.

"Karl," she finally began with poorly dissembled agitation which sent a strange shaking into her usually so calm organs, "I must share something with you. One of your students, Graf Kottop, must not enter our house anymore, do you hear?"

"For God's sake, Lilli, why ever not?"

Then she turned her countenance to me, and I was almost shocked. A force, such a majestic decisiveness sprayed from her dark eyes that I was instinctively horrified before them as though in the presentiment that these features would themselves be fatal to me one day.

"Why?" she repeated stronger, "Karl, that you don't need to ask. It is enough that I have reprimanded him, sharply and with cause, and that you no longer receive him in our house."

So decisively did she issue all this that I stood before her numb and wordless.

Once more I attempted to ask her, but Lilli steered, more impenetrably than usual, immediately onto other subjects, and soon after left my room.

Then I sat, and clutched my head. Just what could she have encountered?

Would this frivolous aristocrat really have dared to affront the wife of Professor Barkentin? Certainly, her husband was absent, was almost never in attendance in the circle in which his wondrous wife was celebrated. An inner fear seized me, became larger and more goading, and would not let my pages hold me any longer.

No, no! The unease grew and swelled. I pushed the book away from me, unconsciously opened the door which led into the adjoining living room, and rushed through our entire apartment, always just driven by an urge to be near my wife.

"Lilli," I cried, "Lilli!"

It was the first time in a long time that I had searched for her.

I found her in the bedroom. She was sitting half undressed by the window, huddled up on a stool, and looking out on the snow covered courtyard. The moon was throwing its bluish light on the thick snow, and also sending a reflection onto my wife's countenance.

She was quite calm. With my entrance, she did not move her head once.

A strange awe held me back from approaching her in a somehow pressing or inquiring manner. She also did not reveal in any way a great agitation.

"Lilli," I began after some time, as I leant by the stove, "are you alright again?"

"Yes," she responded curtly.

Then I did not dare question her further.

And silence reigned between us. And outside in the blue glow of the moon, thick heavy snow flakes were falling down to earth.

VIII

With terrible storms like are only known at sea, February came into land.

From the sea, it howled in as if a gruesome monster was roaring there for its supper. You heard daily of ships' misfortunes. It groaned in the chimneys, and the snowstorm travelled inalterably through the streets.

I know now that this furious hurricane was singing the first jarring tones of the song of my misfortune.

I still think often of that winter evening in which this first became clear to me.

We were sitting down for a supper at which, aside from me and my wife, my mother and Uncle Holm were taking part, when the door opened and my father-in-law entered with his measured greeting. The hour was unusual for him. He tended usually to never come so late. Even Lilli must have noticed something conspicuous in her father's behaviour, for I saw how she followed the merchant anxiously with her eyes.

"Won't you sit down with us, father?" she demanded of him, and set a place for him.

Only the merchant declined everything, and placed himself silently before the iced-up window so as to be able to look down through a peek hole at the frozen harbour.

"You're very quiet? You haven't caught the accursed influenza?" Uncle Holm rasped, displaying constantly a benign interest in the merchant.

The man addressed still remained silent.

I had quite distinctly the feeling that some calamity was gathering near. But that my own destruction was creeping nearer, I still did not comprehend.

Finally my father-in-law turned around.

And strangely, he talked directly to the old ship's captain to whom he had otherwise seldom paid attention.

"Are you of the view," he asked him curtly, "that this hurricane will last a long while yet?"

Uncle Holm laid down his knife and fork, wiped his mouth, and also stared at the iced-up window.

"A long while yet?" he repeated. "Mr Karström, I tell you, when the wind blows out of the accursed storm hole of Wiek, like today, then it'll make its music for at least four weeks."

"Yes, yes," the merchant snapped, "they say that at the shipping company too."

And suddenly, whilst he was looking motionlessly at the floor, something boiled up out of his inner unease, "My largest steamship is overdue. — By five days already. — 200 passengers. — The 'Pride of Pomerania' which cost me millions. — And that ship is barely insured for half that."

He brushed his forehead a few times, and I saw how the entire figure of this usually so indomitable man hunched as if an iron fist lay on his neck. The cold grey eyes strayed from one thing to the next until they again seemed sucked fast to the floor.

"250 human lives," rang out abruptly from his chest.

It sounded like a groan.

I had never thought that the man could take a lively, sympathetic interest in something. That day he thereby became almost human.

Commiserating, I rose and attempted to grasp his hand. But he just made a parrying motion.

"Perhaps the steamer has reached a protective harbour though," I attempted to console Lilli's father. Only this view elicited just a pitying shrug from the shipowner.

"We live in the world of the telegraph," he noted shortly. "In that case, there would have been news long ago. – No, no, the ship is located on the open sea."

"Agreed," Uncle Holm confirmed, and stood up ponderously. "A mishap might have occurred with the engines, or –," he scratched behind his ear, and spoke the following in a low voice, "the spruce ship has gone under with man and mouse."

"Yes," the ship owner concluded darkly.

And as though in mockery, the dull roar of the storm rang in from outside. Roof tiles clattered onto the street, and the shutters of the houses opposite were thrown crashing to and fro.

My father-in-law had sat down at the table. The conversation crept on only falteringly.

Lilli sat herself next to her father, and stroked his smoothly combed, grey blond hair tenderly.

"Who is the captain leading this ship?" she inquired softly.

And then I heard the name for the second time.

"Jensen – he is still young – I hold him to be very capable – but –," the merchant straightened up, and his slack features became firm and energetic again like previously. "We want to talk about something else. By the way, I would like to ask you all to let nothing of the mishap be reported in public. – I don't want the newspapers to engage themselves with it prematurely. Right?"

Shortly thereafter, my father-in-law rose and left.

— — —

In the night, I heard Lilli breathing deeply and moaning several times.

"What's the matter, Lilli?"

"I – I was dreaming – about the ship," she stammered.

And yet her soul was at the time still pure and spotless.

***

Oh, what an egotist the demon housed in the monk's great folio made out of me. Even then, when the sea screamed and ranted wilder daily, when the people in the town already began to stick their heads together to mutter about the great shipping calamity which affected all of us, even in that period, only songs, verses, and rhymes were humming through my brain. – I lived behind a pig leather wall, and considered myself fortunate if I found a fitting translation.

But the upsetting event began to alarm every circle. Even at the university, I heard it talked about, the students stood around in groups, and discussed the for and against, many had an acquaintance on the ship, and everyone was irritated by the uncertainty, the mystery which surrounded the missing vessel.

And in all this furtive excitement, I, unworldly fool, held lectures for my students over decayed things which had nothing in common with life anymore. Yes, I began gradually to become annoyed that there should be concerns in the world which could heat the spirits more than old legends and nordic symbols.

Oh, if I had not been so caught up, then I would have had to have also noticed how in my own house a strangely trembling unease began to stir. My beautiful wife lost a part of her proud measuredness, she was no longer capable of sticking to an activity or holding her place for very long. Even in the biting cold, she frequently opened the window and leant far out to observe the direction of the wind. Then she grasped the newspaper again, and sought feverishly for weather forecasts and news of ships.

I do not know if this strange interest in something unfamiliar, alien to me, began to harm me, the vain fool. I was indignant that she deprived me of a part of her cares. I even began to lose her calm presence by my work.

One day, I complained about it.

But hardly had Lilli heard the first words than she was already slinging her arms gently as ever around me, and looking at me attentively.

And yet strange. It was to me as if my wife should have been thinking of me and my existence first.

And so she strode ahead of me quickly into my work room. Soon afterwards, she was again sitting in her accustomed place, and I felt as previously that her large eyes were accompanying me incessantly.

Sprier and sprier, I wanted to interest her. A distinct feeling muttered to me that I had to capture her soul again fully and entirely.

I read aloud to her with warmth a few of the Low German verses, and strangely — I did not sense at all in that moment the peculiar connection, that it was, right then, the song of the vikings sinking into the sea, who at night and in the light of the moon circle about the site of their shipwreck.

Then Lilli became impatient with my work for the first time. She interrupted me, something alien befell her thought.

"Have you already heard, Karl," she said quite unexpectedly, "my father has received news."

This interruption, this visible inattentiveness made me quite nervous.

"Over what?" I asked, keeping to myself.

"Think, Karl, it excites me so. A foreign captain arrived at my father's and said that, in the terrible hurricane on the ocean, he had encountered the steamer of Captain Jensen, but an understanding had not been possible with the horrible storm. He only knew that the Pride of Pomerania's had an engine mishap, and was leaking. That was eight days ago; but what has become of the steamer since then, no man knows; presumably it has sunk."

"Well, and?" I threw in-between impatiently.

She stared at me. Obviously she did not comprehend my calmness and my position at all.

"My heart trembles, Karl, I can't think of anything else. I constantly see a ship on waves as high as houses, struggling for its life. It's awful. It seems to me sometimes as if I've found myself on that steamer. Can you imagine that?"

"No," I responded, irritated, while she looked wide-eyed into the distance, and certainly did not hear my answer at all.

"Do you want to hear the rest of the poem now, Lilli?"

The page trembled in my hands.

What disappointment! My wife was already no longer paying attention to my voice, she continued as if I had not spoken at all.

"You know, Karl, your mother had an ugly dream last night. It seemed to her as if the sea was under our windows and slowly rising to the first floor and, out of the distance, an enormous ship was floating directly towards the glass panes. It was becoming larger and larger, more and more massive; mother thought the ship would crush her, and wanted to scream, but just before the window, when she already heard the roaring and snorting, the vessel sank soundlessly into the depths. She heard distinctly the crew still wailing, lamenting, and praying. And think, it straightaway struck twelve from St Mary's. Isn't that strange?"

Then I could not control my injured ego anymore. I threw the page with the poem onto the desk, shifted the chair back violently, and burst out, "All ridiculous imagination. Go now, Lilli, go, you are disturbing me."

Oh, I hoped that with these words she would come flying back to me, caressing and kissing me as she usually did. But strange! My beautiful pale wife rose obediently, and walked out in deep thought. — — —

She was the daughter of a dockyard owner, she was brought up by the sea, her spirit did not dwell with me, but with the struggling ship.

IX

The next day, the capital's newspapers brought news of the result. The Pride of Pomerania had sunk near the Antilles. No human lives were saved.

Finally thus certainty. Death had won, and the sea had swallowed its victims.

The spirits of the sunken floated again over the site of the misfortune just as it was read in my folk songs.

A horror overcomes me on my own remembering of these days.

I seemingly heaved a sigh of relief.

Even if my heart shook full of horror over the great number of lost lives which the ravenous sea gulped down, there was now finally calm again.

The calm of certainty.

My wife would not tremble anymore, would not stare out at the distant sea with eyes torn wide open. I could again return to my songs.

And that I did.

Whilst they held in the town, stricken and shaken, silent masses for the dead, I plunged again with increased zeal into my monk's script.

And again Lilli dwelt with me. And again I entertained the feeling that her pure, clear soul had turned to me anew, and was overflowing fully into my verses.

This agreeable silence continued for quite some time.

Then the door was suddenly thrown open, Professor Wackermann, who had just risen from the sickbed, stumbled in with a thick cloth around his neck, and cried in his enthusiastic, tearaway manner, whilst his dear countenance gleamed with joy, "Karl, Karl, is it not all true?"

Lilli started.

"What isn't true, professor?"

"The Pride of Pomerania is still afloat. Hurray, child!"

The old scholar brushed his hand through his hair, tore the thick, woolen cloth down, and rushed back and forth breathlessly in my room. In his imaginatively rich nature, he found himself apparently in the middle of a undulating sea.

"Here," he said, "look, the County Gazette even sold an extra sheet everywhere. Read, children, read. This splendid fellow, this Captain, has kept his ship together despite storm and stress. An English coal steamer saw him floating just the day before yesterday near the Azores. What do you say? Hurrah, children! I am quite beside myself."

Then my wife rose, rushed to the Professor, grasped his hand, and cried with an excitement I had never heard from her before, "My dear — dear Professor, oh how good what you tell is, oh how good!"

Tears fell down that white countenance, her voice trembled, a shiver seemed to pass over her slender limbs.

Still the pair stood hand in hand, then, under the door overhang, the broad face of Uncle Holm also appeared waving his cap spasmodically.

"Karl — — excuse me, dear young woman, but the excitement sits in my stomach so that I can't otherwise. — — Karl, with broken ship's propeller, the between-decks full of water, and a smashed rudder as well, and with all that, holding out for three weeks, only a German could manage that. Now quick, Karl, get dressed, Professor, give me the honour too, I'm opening a bottle of champagne. Yes, yes, that I am. – We must toast to this Captain. Well? Don't you think?"

***

He did not let me have any peace anymore, the unknown distant man on the sea.

Already at the time, he pressed with his steely, broad-chested figure into my quiet work, unintentionally, unwitting, unassuming, and yet strongly, as if it were his being.

Oh, how I hated him!

The tranquility fled from my little study, the stranger was always being spoken about – "a hero – a German mariner – a man of action," thus fell the catchwords which for me – I do not know why – had something instinctively injurious.

And the more stubbornly I sank into my script, the more intrusive and gossipy the boastful rumours about him forced themselves on me.

For three weeks, he had contended on the wreck with the most horrific hurricane which had been experienced within living memory.

"And how he kept discipline properly – with two hundred passengers in board," Uncle Holm enthused – "that I'd be pleased with."

Ever crazier tales were heard. The newspapers published column length articles about the distinguished Captain and his crew, and finally London papers brought out the most remarkable thing. Jensen had alone, pistol in hand, thrown himself against the wailing, fleeing mob who thought to leave the ship on the lifeboats. – He alone, cold, measured, imposing. A sailor who, becoming rabid before fear of death, wanted to clear off the boat had been knocked flat by him with a powerful punch – and with that, he subjugated the ghastlier beast than the sea, the deathly afraid human crowd.

Thus he had saved the souls entrusted to him.

"An honour to the German name," the London papers themselves wrote, "honour to the steadfast man. With such outstanding material, Germany will join the ranks of the sea-faring nations."

***

I cannot continue writing anymore.

No, no, the praise for this man in my memory still irritates me immeasurably.

I run around in my cell, and must constantly imagine his figure, those broad shoulders, the lean, tough head, and those thin, energetic lips which she kissed.

Which she kissed!

What sort of feeling probably overcame them at the same time?

Ha, if I could now awake her to learn that. And the other thing – to know the other thing that I never discovered.

Sometimes I scream aloud, "Wake up, Lilli, wake up."

But the grave does not answer. Only my warder comes, and stares at me.

Whether my thoughts here could gradually become confused?

Fear of that sometimes shakes me.

I want to return to my book. I want to show that I can subjugate myself, that I am stronger than you think, with more willpower than all of you.

Yes, yes, I want to talk about Jensen again.

Onward!

X

He is there.

My father-in-law gives a reception for him. We are invited.

How sharp my thoughts are; they resemble magnifying glasses, they hide nothing from me, they enlarge everything for me, I, unfortunate man, even know to think precisely of the lowliest things.

This time I had unhesitatingly accompanied Lilli. An infuriating curiosity drove me. I had to see him, examine him, the troublemaker who was interfering in the quiet joy of my work.

"An uneducated man, of course," I thought.

A hundred invitees waited patiently in the hall of the gothic house. An almost festive mood lay over the company. And that irritated me again.

When had my students ever waited so apprehensively and quietly for me, even when I had put many sleepless nights into the explanation of some obscure words? —

"Never," the derisive voice muttered in me.

Next to me stood Lilli, her arm resting firmly on my own. Only I felt that she was not thinking of me; her eyes encircled expectantly the frame of the door through which he had to enter. It was afternoon. In the great room, a mysterious half-darkness reigned.

Then steps were heard in the corridor.

"He – is coming," murmured Lilli.

And despite the twilight, I noticed how the blood slowly climbed into her white cheeks.

She stood there with her body bent forward, with held breath, full of suspense, trembling – haha, almost like a bride waiting yearningly for her loved one.

Or is that all subsequently just a play of my hate-filled, churned up imagination?

The door opened and, by the side of the merchant, as well as a government official from Berlin, sent by the Admiralty, the celebrated man entered.

At first, a gentle exclamation of wonder on all sides.

No, no, there was nothing theatrical, nothing studied, everything was truly unpretentious masculinity. Between both the tail-coated gentlemen, on whose chests every possible order gleamed, the tall figure of the sandy haired man appeared almost too plain.

He was wearing again the dark blue, gold-laced uniform, just like I had seen him the first time; in his hand, he held his flat cap, and in his lean, tough countenance, you could distinctly discern that this great festive reception was painful, yes, it embarrassed him.

A fanfare blown by the military band in attendance blared through the hall. I saw how the young man blushed, and looked impatiently at my father-in-law to see whether the presentation and honour would not soon reach their end.

Even Lilli sighed deeply, almost as though relieved. She had seen him, the first suspense was over.

Then a general introduction. I still feel his hand in mine, and sense once again its firm, warm pressure.

Everything that this man did was short, energetic, and gripping.

The lights of the chandelier sparkled. Everyone sat down to table; Lilli and I were seated directly opposite the guest of honour.

And strange. – What I had predicted, began to be fulfilled. Captain Jensen seemed in fact to have a taciturn, inward looking, yes, as I felt almost with some satisfaction, an unhelpful nature. For he looked constantly during the first while quietly and uninterested down at his plate without paying the slightest attention to his neighbours on the right and left. I also noticed how it visibly touched him unpleasantly when the conversation of those sitting around him turned to him and his actions. Then he threw down a few curt factual words, and while his forehead creased more energetically, he continued to look down earnestly before himself as if he were the most negligible person at this celebration.

And yet he naturally formed the point of aim for every glance.

Even Lilli barely let him out of her eye for a moment.

She watched him constantly, goggling as if he were the fulfilment and materialisation of a dream which, always returning, had frightened her soul for months.

But this self-absorption in a strange personality began to hurt me, directly hurt me – to really martyr me spiritually. From the first moment on, I felt a foreboding, consuming jealously towards this quiet, innocent man.

The old monk, who had written his folio in the Cistercian Abbey for me, had flown away out of my thoughts, I just looked ceaselessly at my wife who seemed to me as luminous and beautiful in her inner excitement as I had never seen her before.

I collected all my powers to steer her attention to me.

I set a displaced bow of her dress right on her shoulder. I endeavoured, quite against my nature, to whisper little obscenities about the party into her ear. I broke the conversation of those sitting around me, and finally grasped my glass to say cheers with Lilli.

"The most beautiful woman of those gathered at the table!" I said softly.

Though Lilli did indeed incline her goblet towards me, she did not look at me. For in the same moment as our glasses chimed against each other, Jensen had also straightened up his head, and contemplated my wife for the first time.

Lilli did not turn her eyes away either.

How firmly she still held her glass against mine.

In the strange light grey eyes of the mariner, there was a running here and there as if seeking, recalling something. Finally his pupils lit up, he must have found it. And neither let their eyes off each other, firm and scanning, as if they were speaking to one another.

An unease ran through me like I had never known before. I smiled, but my entire being suddenly seemed spellbound in its ability to be able to unravel this furtive silent interrelation between the two.

No, no, I was deluding myself, must have unmistakably gone astray, it was not possible with my pure, devoted, supportive wife. What could this perfect stranger be to her?

I could not endure it any longer.

I had to speak to him. It seemed to me as if I now had to pitch a battle for my wife, fight out a duel.

And then — then it was suddenly silent in the hall.

The representative of the Admiralty rose, and expressed in the name of the government its thanks to the brave mariner returned home. The entire land was proud of his deed. The ruler himself had followed the eventful fate of the endangered vessel with pounding heart. Now the Prince was compelled to also give a sign of recognition to the distinguished Captain, and hence he — the government official — was commissioned with presenting to Captain Jensen this high order. He closed with a cheer for the excellent representative of German seafaring, for the teacher, and the example of his crew.

"In the name of the Emperor! Hooray! Hooray! Hooray!"

It came over the entire gathering like a frenzy. A fanfare blew exultantly through the hall.

With quick excited steps, the gentleman from the government approached the home comer, who slowly raised his lowered head, and presented him with a small box in which the distinction was contained.

Then Lilli clasped my arm as if she had something to whisper to me. But she said nothing — nothing at all. — Her chest rose and fell feverishly, the general excitement had drawn her with it into its swirling stream. Her otherwise so marmoreal, white cheeks glowed brightly.

And again an almost frightening silence occurred. The Captain had remained standing behind his chair, you knew that he would respond to the government official.

Gentlemen and ladies rise in order to see him. Everyone hangs on his lips. Really, this silent certainty has something dominant, subjugating about it.

He begins.

What he says is absolutely nothing unusual, the words even sound sober and dry, and yet these tersely ejaculated syllables sound like rifle shots passing sharply and thrillingly over the many heads.

He concludes, "All thanks, from wherever it comes, I must decline. No human being wants to perish before his time. I was only defending myself. Anyone would do that. That it was possible for me though –"

And here – here he turns his head, and looks under his red bushy eyebrows down directly at my wife, as if they both find themselves entirely alone in a secluded room, as if he has a confession to make to her falteringly and reluctantly.

"That it was possible for me though, this successful defence against death, that I alone owe to the excellence of the vessel which was entrusted to me. It was built in the Karström's dockyards. Every nail was banged in by German industry and German intelligence. It is thus German work which won victory on the sea. – The house of Karström, the seat of German solidarity and efficiency, let it blossom further in all its branches and for all eternity!"

His voice sounded at the end quite soft, as if he were sharing everything personally with my wife. And as if it were something obvious, he also stretched his glass over the table to her first.

Everyone rose, everyone cheered, and waved. The glasses clinked, the music was jubilant.

Then my wife also straightened up slowly. The eyes of the mariner glided in honest admiration over her figure. Nothing disrespectful lay in his behaviour, he just held the glass motionless in his calm hand towards her.

And then she bent forward, and clinked glasses with him.

I would have liked to have pulled back her arm. Already at the time, a mad, distasteful feeling was creeping up on me, as if I had been thrown to the ground, and was being trampled on — —. The blood climbed humming into my head. I could not have lasted any longer at all in my place at the side of my wife, whose eyes were beaming so brightly like they had not done for months.

Thank God! My father-in-law then rose, the reception was at an end.

***

I spoke with him.

An impregnable desire drove me constantly into his proximity.

Once more I looked around; Lilli was sitting in conversation with other ladies, almost separated from us by the entire length of the hall. Like in flight, my eyes remained fastened on the wonderful, white skin of her neck.

I spoke with him.

Under the wide bayed window niche, he stood in a circle of gentlemen and ladies. Each man clustered to catch a word from the brave man, the young ladies timidly presented him their fans for him to autograph.

But Jensen declined all this with his candid smile.

"No, no, my ladies," he defended himself, "I don't like to make myself ridiculous, you yourselves will realise that later."

Only a few of the older officers as well as Professor Wackermann, who stood around him chattering, were given terse and modest answers to short and sober questions.

I joined them, and soon we were in conversation.

And strange! His calm manner had something agreeable to it which shackled me instinctively.

"Now you will certainly remain home for a long time," I asked, "to rest yourself, won't you?"

I think something was lurking hidden in my tone.

Meanwhile, Jensen shook his head.

"No, Professor," he responded, "I will only stay here a short while."

I sighed.

"Will you not return then to my father-in-law's shipping company?" I inquired further.

He also answered that in the negative.

"The Norwegian polar expedition have shown me the honour of choosing me as leader of their newly built steamer. I have accepted it. I have been once before in the Arctic Circle, and long to return there."

Then Professor Wackermann struck him enthusiastically on the shoulder.

"You want to open the eternal gates of ice, Captain?" he cried with his wistful grin.

"Yes," the latter replied, "I want to help with that."

And now, with the recollection of his journey and the northern sea, he began to lose some of his reserve, and surprised us by the warm, animated manner of his description.

"Karl," Wackermann whispered to me, "that is half a scholar, what a remarkable man!"

And even I was captured. This pronounced scholarly interest which streamed from the man, for which he was even ready to put his life on the line for, made him appear to me like one of us.

My hate, my ridiculous envy flickered for only a moment. I offered him my hand, and while he shook it strongly and sincerely, I invited him, with a strangely contradictory feeling, to regard my house as his own as long as he still remained in our town.

"I possess many geographic maps," I explained to him, "surely you love rare works as well?"

Then that bright gleam again ran over the reserved countenance, he fetched a deep breath.

"Yes," he said simply, "books form my relaxation. If you allow, I will join with you and your set of friends."

And once more, we shook one another's hands.

***

I travelled home with Lilli.

In the carriage, it occurred to me that she was chattering as thrilled and happy as seldom ever.

I did not know why I had to observe her constantly.

In particular, from this pernicious moment on, I acted like a spy who lay in wait for something hostile.

Why did she just constantly recount, and present questions to me without waiting for my answers?

Gently singing, she tapped at the same time on the panes of the carriage.

"Did you entertain yourself, Karl?" she finally asked, leaning back to me, and slung her interlocked hands around my shoulders so that her slender, young body hung on me.

Oh, now it was time! – Once more, I would have given in, once more, I would have had to embrace her and pull her to me, before the power which was already stretching its hand to her necessarily and compulsively had fully taken possession of her.

But my heart was full of offended self-gloom.

I gave no response to her question. – I, ridiculous fool, thought to punish her through silence and holding back for her neglect of me.

Oh God! How bloodily I had to atone for it!

XI

A few days later. Outside a bitter frost reigned so that towards evening in my study, large pieces of wood had to be burnt in the stove. They jerked and crackled agreeably through the still silence.

I sat and worked, joyless and distracted, for my thoughts did not reside in my work anymore.

Woe, woe! I had not known that previously. Our work desires absolute devotion, meanwhile something disturbing was persistently running through my mind. I had to constantly think of my wife, who in the previous days had lived there so cheerfully and tidily, and seemed not once to sense in her naive cheerfulness that I was daily becoming more taciturn and depressed.

I hesitated — — — what was that?

Inside, my wife was singing, in a low voice but brightly and jovially.

"Lilli — Lilli," I sighed instinctively, while I propped both arms on the folio to bury my aching head in my hands.

And suddenly I started. Yes, that was it. Now I had finally found a name for the feeling which was cutting through me so painfully, which tormented me and drove away my ease. — — — I felt fear, fear before the woman to whom I had bound myself and whom I did not know.

Something I had read in my books by inimical philosophers occurred to me: The woman is something unrecognised, threatening, which from the outset plans on annihilation; she is the seducer of this world, who carries before herself a cheerful and dangerous mask.

Oh, this ridiculous and yet so tormenting suspicion, what could the singing wife be up to in there? And why is she so cheerful? Whether the robust tall man was really to blame for all that? "But," it screamed in me, "she loved you, she proved it to you daily — —"

And then the still uglier distrust trickled through me unexpectedly, that which had ruled me from the outset and which had only been silenced by Lilli's openly shown affection over months. The cutting, shaking fear that I was too little for her, too weak of life and will, and that she could perhaps be derisive of the fusty scholar buried under books.

Only now did the thought come to me.

In total confusion, I rose, and crept into the corner of my room where the little plush canopied mirror gleamed. I wanted to see myself. To laugh at myself.

I stared into it.

A pale countenance with mild eyes radiated back to me, a lanky body which the force of life had to overwhelm.

Oh, the pain of this knowledge was unspeakable.

No, no, I could not endure this torment. I could not do without what I had once possessed, I was so accustomed to love, starting from my mother.

Then I heard ringing, then a pair of muffled voices in the adjoining room. I distinctly heard the deep, pithy organ which followed me into my dreams, and next to it Lilli's agreeable voice. My heart pounded to bursting.

He was here.

Whether he would stay long with her?

But no, the portière was already pulled back, and with a powerful 'good evening', Jensen entered.

Behind him, I perceived for a moment the figure of my wife, the we found ourselves alone.

Astonished and taken aback, he looked around with me. The rich comfort of my room seemed to touch him pleasantly.

"You have it very nice here," he said finally with his deep voice, which itself exercised on me a quite peculiarly subjugating effect, "very nice, really, so sequestered and calm."

"And that pleases you, Captain?" I asked timidly.

He had turned to my bookcases so that the tall figure now had its back turned to me, and he responded airily over his shoulder, "Yes, Professor, as strange as it sounds from a mariner, I love calm and solitude above all else. Hence why I'm joining the polar expedition."

"Mind you, the silence which you find there must be majestic."

He nodded, and turned back to me again.

When he was standing next to me, he had to look down to me. His bright eyes were still examining the furniture of my scholarly room.

"Yes, yes, previously such a little room, full of books and rare maps, was also my wish," he began, while he sat down to the side of my desk so that his blond head was illuminated brightly by my lamp.

Again the exceptional honesty of his features surprised me, and something muttered in me, 'The great betrayal which you predict can not come to you from this man.'

Oh, I so wanted to breath easy.

"Yes, such a little room was my wish," he continued. "You see, Professor, I'm the son of the Pastor of a little fishing village up by Darst. When I was still riding on my father's knee, I was likewise surrounded by such folios. It sticks in the blood."

"And yet you did not become a scholar?" I inquired half indifferently.

My eyes had to constantly measure the tall broad shouldered figure as if I were waiting for it to rise and aim a blow at me.

It was sheer madness. And yet such an unsuspecting truth lay at the bottom of it all.

"And yet you did not become a scholar?"

"No, you know of course, the great flood came, half of my native island sank into the sea, my father, mother, and sisters drowned, I myself was pulled from the water by a compassionate fisherman. Then I was sent to the mariner's school at the state's cost. And thus I am what I now am."

Whilst we thus conversed, I had ignored that there had been a light knock on the door. Now the portière rustled, and Lilli stuck her blond head in.

"Is it permitted?" she asked as was her habit, whilst she remained for a while in her picturesque pose, the heavy curtain pulled back with her outstretched hand.

Jensen barely turned. That attracted my attention. The figure in the doorframe appeared to me, however, like the image of a wonderful nymph seemingly calling for love.

With trembling voice, I requested she step closer. And soon she was sitting in her brown leather armchair by the stove, and her first question was along the lines of whether the Captain would not like to have supper with us?

In my dull indifference, I wondered only weakly that she did this so independently, and yet I repeated her request.

Simply and heartily, the mariner expressed his willingness, and then a short pause of self-consciousness occurred between us three.

It was like the quiet before the storm.

I observed them both.

Lilli had reclined her slender body, and slung both hands behind her head. She thereby lifted her breasts. She kept her eyes, pointed in the direction of our guest, half shut as if she were dreaming or expecting something arresting, something tantalising to think about.

And even Jensen, who still remained turned to me under the beam of the lamp, seemed to sense something similar, for he unexpectedly picked up the thread of the torn conversation again.

"Yes," he repeated thoughtfully, "father – mother – sisters drowned – my home deep under water – there is probably some such similar thing in your folk songs, Professor – so it's no wonder I learnt to treasure solitude!

Then Lilli sighed heavily.

"You experienced that?" she murmured still with her eyes shut. "And now you have no friend, Captain?"

The latter did not stir.

"No," fell tersely from his lips, "none, only a girlfriend."

That startled me.

"A girlfriend?" I inquired tensely.

"The sea," he replied with a gently melancholy smile.

Lilli stirred.

I saw how her eyes opened to encompass fully the man who was turned away from her.

"The sea that has robbed so much from you?" she asked softly. "How is that possible?"

Now Jensen altered his position, and looked over at the woman sitting in the half shadows.

"You know well, Mrs Barkentin," he conveyed slowly, and it seemed to me as if his words sounded less certain now than before, "You know well that we mariners possess a superstitious trait. So it is with me too. I must travel out to sea because it is for me sometimes as if I were finding something out there. Perhaps my sisters, perhaps my home. In any case, something that I am missing. You may laugh over that, but the sea lies before me like something dark, uncertain, and it often seems to me as if it thus only calls me so loud to preserve me from a calamity on land. For we mariners don't merely sink in the seas."

For a while, it remained silent between us.

Opposite this childish superstition, I suddenly won back my inner superiority. Almost pityingly, I smiled over at Lilli, as if I wanted to invite her to likewise agree with my derision. But, oh horror, my wife was staring at the strange man as if he had drawn back the veil of something supernatural for her.

I absolutely could not comprehend all that, and annoyed, only subjugating myself with effort, I rose, pulled back the portière and saw that the table in the adjoining room had been laid.

"I invite you!" I requested quite curtly.

***

I still hear her singing.

For the first time in a long time, Lilli had sat down at the piano and made music.

Her tones had something dark, urgent from the innermost soul. That day the passion which was voiced out of these depths appeared doubly strange to me. Even the love's laments she sung had something threatening about them.

My mother, who had shared supper with us, sat next to me, and had seized me by the hand. The old woman looked stiffly at the face of the strange mariner who reclined opposite us at the illuminated table looking thoughtfully and seriously over at Lilli.

Then the old woman turned again to my wife, and seemed to be listening fearfully to her voice.

Instinctively I had to follow all the movements of my mother.

Had she also become uneasy?

Strange – strange! She was stroking me incessantly on the arm as if a wrong had been done to me – her only one.

Oh, you dear old woman!

Finally Lilli leant back.

She hardly heard what the stranger said to her in thanks, she kept her eyes shut as if she had completely expended herself, and was now silent from exhaustion.

This outburst, this ecstatic style was otherwise altogether foreign to her.

It became ever quieter, uncomfortableness began to intrude on us from every corner of the room, until even the Captain, quietly thinking to himself, was seized by it, stood up quickly, and offered me his hand in parting.

When he gave his regards to Lilli, she offered him her fingers curtly, almost indifferently, and drew them straight back hastily.

It all attracted my attention. I observed it all. I lay in wait like a starved fox.

On parting, almost already standing in the doorway, Jensen unbuttoned his coat as if he were pondering something, and pulled out a longish object wrapped in tissue paper.

"Right," he remembered, "I brought this along with me for you, Professor. I ask that you accept it from me."

He removed the covering. It was an antique, double-edged dagger, made from copper, with a yellow ivory handle from which gleamed a blood-red ruby in the form of an eye.

"I bought it in Buenos Aires as a rarity," the mariner explained. "It is meant to be an ancient American weapon. This eye indicates heathen origins. Take it, Professor, it will give you delight."

Tall and towering, he stood in the doorway.

But the desire for all that was dead, decayed, and past gripped me. My hand twitched to the weapon, and held it delightedly up to the light.

The ruby sparkled as if the eye were crying a bloody drop.

XII

Like an eerie, black shadow which creeps along the walls, the fear drove me before it.

It mixed into all the motions of my life. It even intruded into the protective walls of the university to scare me.

An upsetting, horrible incident is memorable to me. — — — On the day after the Captain's visit, I held my usual lecture in one of the elongated lecture halls of the college.

I sat at the lectern and recited to my students a few of the songs of old minstrels.

Exactly as I was feeling the harmony of the verses, I perceived how the many young eyes were directed interested as me, I heard the scratching of pens transcribing.

Suddenly — like lightning, the word escapes me — I seek, cannot find, I turn here and there, the horror presses my heart into my mouth. Finally — finally I stammer out the sought after expression, but the flow of my talk is interrupted; I cannot collect myself, instead the old chivalrous singers are unforeseen the figures of my wife and the stranger who follows me constantly, stepping before my soul, and these two do not let go of my thoughts anymore.

I continue speaking, but I confuse myself. I see only Jensen and my wife. The blood shoots into my face. My students become restive, they become astonished at me — then I pull together my last strength, rise, and after I have incoherently made a pretext of a sudden unwellness, I run trembling out of the lecture hall, and flee homeward.

***

I kept this mood silent from my wife. I was ashamed to be sick and not in command of my body so like the other man. I had to constantly think of his tall, muscular figure, of his steely limbs.

And Lilli did not notice my strange, trembling unwinding at all. She only threw a long look at me when she saw me walking through the room on my return that day. And I was so mad already, so hounded and discouraged, that I imagined something like derision, at a minimum something evaluating and comparing, was in her look.

Dead tired, I collapsed at my desk in the afternoon. I could not work. Only leaf through the great monk's script, leaf, and peer out unthinking through the steamed up windowpanes.

Professor Wackermann encountered me thus as he stepped into the darkness to see me around the fifth hour. He started when he saw me slouched in this darkness.

"Karl, what are you doing?"

"I – I – I'm not quite well."

"So make some light."

"Yes – yes – certainly – straightaway."

When I had hastily lit the lamp, the old man remained standing before me. Then he adjusted his blue glasses, and finally burst out worried, "You look really pale, Karl. Tell me, boy, you're not getting something serious?"

"Eh keep calm," I comforted him, "nothing serious at all."

Shaking his head, the old gentleman sat down close by me, and grasped my hand, which he caressed affectionately. He still seemed to be worried, for he, exceptionally, did not speak immediately about our work.

"Karl, tell me, why are you sitting here so alone?" he began after a pause, still stroking me.

"Alone?" I stuttered. "My wife has gone to my father-in-law's."

The old man nodded a few times, and remained silent for a while. Then he said calmly – certainly without thinking anything of it, "She'll meet Jensen there."

"Jensen?"

There it was.

I closed my eyes, fetched a deep breath, and clutched the arms of my chair. It penetrated me as if someone had stabbed me with a knife. Something cut through my pounding heart so that I would have liked to have whimpered aloud, and only with extreme force was I capable of bursting out, "Have you met – him?"

"Yes, I saw him entering the house."

"And – and my wife too?"

"That I don't know. – That you said yourself before, Karl."

"Oh yes – that – quite right – I said that."

Silence again occurred between us for a while. I collapsed into my armchair, and struggled for air. If I had just once been able to groan, strike my forehead and scream, but the presence of my old friend robbed me of this mercy. Certainly, my brain was brewing ever madder images. Thus now the two were in the gothic house alone. Now it could already have happened. Whether they who were meant for each other had already found themselves? And whether they now mocked me and my impotence?

A gentle sigh forced itself over my lips. My irritable imagination conjured ever more fervent images before me. I seemingly became intoxicated in the caresses which the two could be exchanging with each other.

Now Jensen would be carrying her in his arms, lifting her high above the ground, and carrying her. He possessed the strength for rocking this grown-up woman in the air like a child. Now she would be slinging her arms around his neck, those glorious, full arms. – – –

Oh God – – –

"Karl," Wackermann murmured, and shook me by the arm. "Nothing will happen with the work today. Shall I – shall I not inform your wife?"

Yes, yes, that was deliverance. The pair must be separated, chased apart before the sin ripens.

"Yes, yes, dear friend, I beg you, call my wife, inform her – I am – I am – –"

Then I faltered.

No, no, how might I then? I must not concede that I was ailing, that I was not as robust as the other man. The air of sickness must not stream from me, that could frighten away from me completely my beautiful wife who thirsts after health.

I grasped my forehead, and slowly straightened up. "Already over," I murmured. "I don't want to scare my wife – no, it is best that I lie down and rest a little. – Just a little rest."

My friend seemed to have wished for something similar himself. Animatedly he nodded, and looked around the room restively. Then he asked me if I would like to lie down straightaway. Only when I had firmly promised him this did he decide on the departure which I desired so much.

On parting, he wanted to say something else comforting to me.

"Tomorrow, Karl," he encouraged, while he bound his thick, woolen scarf around his neck, "tomorrow we will continue our work, won't we? – The old monastic lord could become ungracious to us otherwise."

At the same time, he tapped affectionately on the massive, yellow folio.

But my heart was not attached anymore to my old idols. "No – no," I tossed out indifferently, "not tomorrow — — not the day after tomorrow either — — I will write to you, dear colleague."

The old man stood still, and measured me with a curious, mournful look.

Did he notice that I was shying away from our scholarship, that an aversion was slowly rising in me before these yellow pages, that I wanted to know nothing, and felt nothing but the torment over my wife who was turned away from me?

"Take care, Karl," he said softly, and looked at the floor, "get well soon."

"Good evening, dear Wackermann."

He left.

I remained alone, and pondered. Mechanically, I let myself sink into the armchair by the stove in which usually Lilli always rested, and stared before me.

What now?

End and beginning of all thoughts which tormented me, the idea constantly formed recurrently, "You are ugly, small, powerless, withered in the dry heat of your study; the other man, however, is self-assured, formed from marrow and iron. Life originates in him, from you death."

Oh, how the scorn for myself consumed me, how it gnawed at me, how it bit away from me piece by piece what had adorned my life until then.

So wretched did I seem to myself, so neglected and betrayed by nature, so ripe for being cast off and disowned.

Whether that now soon stood before me? And when would the moment occur? For Lilli would not disappoint me, that I knew. As soon as she was clear about it, she would come to me with the request. How much respite was I still allowed? Oh, the fear of this moment made a loud racket in my heart, and made my breath falter.

No, no, just not this uncertainty. I demand nothing more of her, nothing further from my beautiful, ardently loved wife but clarity – clarity and certainty.

Suddenly I started.

There was a ringing. – Lilli's voice. – –

Then I knew it. I wanted to ask her. I wanted to force her to answer me.

Forthwith – immediately!

***

"Isn't mother with you?" Lilli asked taken aback when she entered my room.

She was unbuttoning her fur jacket.

"The weather is becoming milder outside, Karl," she continued, gliding into the armchair and shaking the snowflakes off her skirt. "Proper sledding temperature."

How lithe all her movements were. Yes, yes, she had come from him. Her lips were glowing as if they had been kissed with wild passion.

I stood before her, and noted all that. And yet no indignation rose in me, in me still lived the entire force of the divorce, the apprehension that I would perhaps soon have to separate from her. At the time, I still would have liked to fall down before her, embrace her knees, and beg for mercy.

So little filled with hate, so powerless, I thought at that time. But I got a grip on myself.

I had to ask her. Create clarity. Dispel the lies.

I made ready.

"Did you – did you meet Jensen?"

My voice sounded quite different than usual. Yet it did not attract my wife's attention. Completely ingenuously, rocking back and forth animatedly, she nodded eagerly.

"Dear – of course – he gave his regards," she chattered as though in smiling recollection, and took off her beret. A few snowflakes still shimmered on her golden hair.

The sparkling strands seemed dishevelled to me. Oh, my calamitous imagination hounded me ever deeper into ruin.

Or had I at the time already seen correctly?

My wife kept smiling always quite happily, and rocked like a contented child.

"Karl, dear, I have a request for you."

"A request?"

I was thrown into confusion. Her tone sounded as pure and ingratiating as ever. Should I really put the decisive question now?

I hesitated.

"Dear" – she grasped my hand while her eyes sparkled ceaselessly into the distance. "We will make a trip on an ice yacht tomorrow. Yes? To Rügen. The Captain has invited us. Please, please, Karl, come with me. Do me the pleasure, think please, I have never sat in an ice yacht, and am looking forward to it like a child. Jensen owns his own boat. – Will you? Say yes."

I stood there, and stared at her.

The sweat was coming through all my pores. I noticed how her entire soul hung on the trip, I knew that this overt joy in being together with the stranger enclosed something harmful for me, and yet – and yet – everything in her worked on me so innocently, so openly, so pristinely.

Oh thanks – thanks, a thousand thanks, she must still have been blameless. Only the completed betrayal could otherwise express itself so harmless and childlike, no, no, Lilli was pure, up to then everything was certainly still playful, rambling wish. Of course, now I had to surround her, hold her fast, ensnare her with threefold love.

And from here on begins the most deplorable chapter of my existence. I began to abase myself before her. To the woman who was pleased by bold strength, I crept like a lady's maid.

Gently I caressed the dreaming woman's sparkling hair.

"Lilli, did Jensen also invite me?"

"You?"

She turned her head. It seemed to me as if she had to think to herself. "Of course. How did you come to that? – And don't you think we could assume that?" she asked further excitedly, and grasped my hand warmly. "Don't you think we could assume that?"

Mechanically I nodded. Everything was so turbid around me, I felt no foothold anywhere; so I surrendered irresolutely to my fate.

"Okay, Lilli," I murmured, "if it offers you joy."

Then she sprang up. Her chest expanded. "So then, tomorrow afternoon at two o'clock!" she cried, barely containing herself.

Again I hesitated.

Did she know then that my seminar students gathered with me at this time? Did my scholarship count for nothing, nothing at all anymore?

"Oh, then call it off for once, Karl," she rebutted as if she had guessed my thoughts. "Look, you don't want to trouble us! Well?"

She brushed with her arm over my shoulder at the same time, probably half unintentionally. But seared through me as if it had been a caress.

I still thirsted then after the smallest offering.

"If you think," I stammered obediently.

She now really leant on me.

"Oh, that is nice of you, Karl," she cried quite joyfully, "really nice," and suddenly she grasped my head with both hands, and I felt a pair of hot lips on my cheek.

This hot glow! — — — these wonderfully soft lips! — — —

If only the wild sneering voice had not been in my inner being, which cried loudly, "Do not cradle yourself in hope, while she kisses you, she is thinking of the other man. All your folios will not conquer the glowing, yearning body of the woman. She is compelled away from you — to the stranger, to the stronger man. — It only remains for you to step aside — to give up."

"Come, Karl," Lilli demanded, perplexed, "we'll go to mother."

The night which I spent was tormenting. — Next to me, my breathing wife, and in me, this snakes' nest of doubts. Unnoticed, I often bent over her to observe her. The moon fell brightly on her countenance, and she lay calmly marble-like, and — smiled.

Oh this puzzle, this appalling pain.

XIII

Karl, now climb in," Uncle Holm wheezed, standing below on the iced-up harbour steps, while he winked up at me with his face angry red.

We had encountered the old man on the previous evening with my mother, and in his harmless obtrusiveness, he had immediately offered to accompany us.

Now he was hobbling next to Captain Jensen in massive fur boots around the great ice boat, and tapping the brown horse, which would pull us out to the open sea, good-naturedly on the neck and muzzle.

Meanwhile I climbed cautiously down the smooth steps with Lilli, her arm laid gently in mine, – how one sometimes recalls a triviality – I suddenly felt how Lilli held my arm back worriedly as if she wanted to protect me from the smoothness of the steps.

"Carefully, Karl," she whispered. "Then you almost fell."

Her eyes dipped for a short moment dark and terrified into mine.

"My God," I thought in my brooding inner strife, "isn't that the same concern she always nurtured for you? Aren't you deceiving yourself?" And straight afterwards, the hostile sentiment again rushed in-between. "Whether she would also have it for the other man who remains so healthy and erect down there in his fur jacket, whether she would also feel for him such an abashed, almost maternal fearfulness that he could tumble over?" – – – – – Jensen stretched out his hand to us to help us with the first step onto the ice. Then he looked towards the sun which was floating reddish over the fields in a grey snowy sky.

"How mild the air is," he commented to Lilli. "Wind and weather have conformed to you, Mrs Barkentin."

In his calm words lay a quiet homage. In his way of lifting her into the sled lay something shaking, coveting, pushed back.

Oh, my senses had sharpened so exceedingly, my mental sense of touch was so sensitive, so nervous, that nothing escaped me anymore.

"Now, Professor," Uncle Holm commanded, appearing now on the boat as well. "Now you sit with your back to the wind! Otherwise harm could come to you. And I have promised mother to take care. Captain, you sit for the time being next to the Professor's wife at the rudder, and I will drive the horse until we are at the bay. Then you can start the sailing for my part. I don't understand any of that. I'll scrabble forwards to the stern."

The commands of the old man were complied with.

Soon the yacht was gliding between the narrow banks of the Ryck, the horse's bell rang softly, and Uncle Holm crouched in his fur at the stern and cracked the whip from time to time.

In quarter of an hour, we had reached the gulf.

The wind had cleared the vast expanse of snow, the ice expanse stretched out mirror smooth and gleaming, it sparkled in the distance like a dark brazen shield. Here the horse was consigned to a fisherman, and Jensen rose to hoist the sail with wheezing Uncle Holm in the middle of the yacht. The wind blew the canvas wall powerfully, and with stunning quickness, the light vessel was flying over the silent tracks like a bird shooting purposefully across the sea.

The movement was so soundless and pleasant, the weather so mild.

Half in awe, I had to look up to the tall young man who sat erectly in the yacht in order to hold the sail's rope with a firm hand.

His arm seemed to know no fatigue. He chattered innocuously with my wife, and brought to her attention the beauties of the winter landscape surrounding us.

There in particular was the snow hill which had formed on the vanishing shore of the bay, which occupied our attention through its fanciful shape.

"Look, Mrs Barkentin," the young mariner said earnestly, "there a temple has seemingly erected itself at the top, with columns and portals, and the red snowy sun is covering the lot with a flickering blue roof. The king of silence could live there."

My wife with her large, wistful eyes looked over earnestly. But I, who had just before smiled over the childishly poetic way this man expressed himself, I was also seized that day by the silent, almost poetic depth of spirit which ran out from the otherwise so modest man. Thoughtfully I stared over at the sparkling temple.

Then Uncle Holm interrupted this strange mood already surrounding us others with his shaggy ribaldry.

"So," he grinned, "for my part, the king of silence can live where he likes. I have here something much more sensible. Look, children, two bottles of rum of the very finest. I'm an old mariner and know what the stomach needs on such a trip."

With that he fetched from both his massive side pockets two large bottles, and uncorked one of them. He did not rest until the rest of us had tasted the drink he idolised.

And again it touched me peculiarly when I saw how Jensen received the mug from Lilli's hands, and emptied it devoutly, his look directed firmly on her.

Again it seemed to me as if he had at the same time directed an ardent speech to her, and Lilli also followed each of his movements with her dark look.

Around us, it was becoming duskier, the sun was red on the distant peaks of the snow covered mountains which we had left behind us. Soundless and arrow-quick, the vessel was now whistling across the open expanse.

Jensen was still sitting and holding the rope with his outstretched hand.

But suddenly Uncle Holm lifted his head, and sniffed about in the air with his nose.

"Do you notice that?" he asked the Captain standing up next to him.

"Yes," Jensen replied, "the wind is veering, it's a nuisance."

And really. Hardly had both mariners exchanged opinions than the sail also flapped slackly on the mast, filled out a few times, and finally hung down still and motionless.

"There you are," Uncle Holm shouted, and he clambered cursing out of the boat while the vessel was barely still moving forward.

"Yes, now just tell me what we do now? I know the story, these dead calms can last for hours. Then we would surely have to overnight here in the yacht! Cheers! Me and my trips! Captain, why didn't you leave me at home!"

And Lilli also began to fret.

"Really?" she asked, while she straightened up, and now also stood next to Jensen. "Must we remain lying here?"

Her glance fell on me, I do not know whether she was fearful for my sake. In any case, I could not suppress a certain schadenfreude that this powerful, self-assured North Pole explorer, whose fame had filled an entire land, now stood before us so powerless and helpless.

"Four o'clock," Uncle Holm murmured apprehensively when he drew a hulking timepiece out of his pocket, and I could abstain from adding, "It's getting darker and darker. We will barely still be able to find the way back."

And actually, all around us, the twilight was prevailing, the sun was escaping, only the snow radiated an uncertain light.

Oh, I would have wished we had all perished there miserably. Frozen and decayed, before I had acquired the certainty of my ruefulness. How happily I would still have died at the time!

But my fate wanted otherwise.

"What now, Captain?" Lilli asked once more, and instinctively laid her hand on Jensen's shoulder.

And as if this touch brought back his old strength, the mariner calmly straightened up, and asked my wife and I to keep our places without worrying.

"An hour yet," he said, "we have until Putbus, the lights you can already see flickering. I will push you till then."

I stare at him to see if he was joking, but in the same moment, the vessel was already moving forwards again, and Jensen was striding behind the yacht pushing, seemingly without particular effort.

"God's lightning, that's an idea," Uncle Holm said, hobbling bent next to him. "If you permit, Captain, then I will also climb in."

With that he sat down next to me, and slowly the vessel glided onward.

My heart pounded. I saw how Lilli turned around to chat with the man who strode so closely behind her.

Oh, how flattering and trembling her voice sounded as she spoke with him. I had not been hearing such sweet tones from her mouth anymore for a long time. Ceaselessly she deplored that he had to strain himself so for our sakes, yes, once she even laid her hand on his fingers to feel whether they had gone numb yet.

I saw how Jensen quite unexpectedly lowered his head as if he were abstaining from kissing the little hand which caressed him.

I saw all that, I felt all that, I noticed all that – and had to remain silent.

It was becoming darker and darker, more and more silent in the yacht. Heavy cold began to penetrate us, I felt how my body and thoughts were slowly turning stiff. I leant firmer against Uncle Holm's fur as he slumbered in gentle rapture next to me, and out of the darkness, I still heard the indistinct murmur of my wife exchanging soft words with our rescuer.

Gradually, however, these two also fell silent. And it became darker and darker. You could finally hear just the steady stride of Jensen and the creaking of the yacht.

Then suddenly something passed across the sea. Thank God! The wind had sprung up, Jensen stepped back into the yacht, trimmed the sail, and was now seated next to my wife.

I thought I felt how she shivered from cold or from passion, and in any case huddled close to the man sitting next to her.

But I did not stir anymore. Even though my inner being gestured so full of hate, the outer cold did not let me come to any movement anymore.

Wistfully my eyes adhered to the flickering lights, becoming ever brighter, which shimmered from the land.

We swished towards them. In grey twilight. Then a violent blow, we had touched land. Right before us, the lit-up beach hotel loomed. We found ourselves exactly before our goal. With astounding certainty, or with almost incomprehensible luck, Jensen had guided us there.

Yes, yes, luck, that was it. He was one of those whom the easy whores ran to beg from.

Oh, what a pleasure trip this had been.

With aching feet and burning forehead, I strolled next to Uncle Holm who crept to the illuminated portal drowsily next to me.

But in front of us, Jensen and Lilli strode. Tall and erect, and joking with one another cheerfully. They were the strong ones, they alone.

XIV

In the hall of the hotel, we sat united together for supper. Jensen had insisted that we be his guests.

The white covered table placed by the enormous stove, a work of art which the landlord, at this late hour, had fed again with massive pieces of wood. Now the flames were crackling high, and throwing their red glow over us.

Shattered, I sat with the others, and again I had to experience the power the hated man exercised over his fellow men. For hardly had Jensen, moving so freshly and alertly as if he had not some time ago been shoving a heavy vessel before himself, shed his fur jacket than the hotel owner with great pleasure shook both hands of the brave mariner whom he had immediately recognised from the illustrated broadsheets, and asked that he might entertain us at his cost.

"It is an honour for me to host Captain Jensen of the Pride of Pomerania under my roof," he declared.

And he would not let himself be refused.

Soon the table abounded with the most select northern dishes; the hotel owner, who had sat down with us, had his oldest wine brought out, and in the end, a foaming champagne was pouring down our throats.

And here in the long, white hall in which our words echoed loudly, the irrevocable certainty came to me that I had lost that day my sweet wife, my fortune.

It was as if nothing more existed for her except him. She lived and moved still under his eyes, her gently open lips seemed to whisper inaudible greetings over to him. The desire enclosed in her soul was expressing itself more and more truly and blatantly.

Something impelling and lithe which I had never noticed before came into her entire posture.

And strange! Even Uncle Holm was much more taciturn than usual. Admittedly, the old mariner was downing glass after glass of the heady champagne, but beside that, he propped his head in his powerful fist, and blinked, seemingly sleepy, over at the other two.

From time to time, he shook his head imperceptibly.

"Want to go sleep, Karl," he finally murmured vaguely to himself, and pushed his glass away from himself, "I think, now it's time."

And while Lilli and the Captain still remained before the great stove, and bent together over the huge hearth as if they wanted to warm themselves, Uncle Holm plucked a few times energetically at his coat.

"Come, my boy!"

Numbed by wine and my torment, I did not follow straightaway. Then he placed his fist in my side, and whispered again a more urgent "come".

With his hulking head, he nodded to the door at the same time.

Unnoticed, I followed him.

My wife and the strange mariner were still letting the reddish glow of the stove wash around them, in silence, and yet as if they were relishing a long yearned for pleasure.

I felt it all.

Outside in the open hallway in which the sea wind whistled in loudly, Uncle Holm detained me, and twiddled a button on his coat self-consciously.

The honourable old man was the one from whose mouth my fate was first reported to me in its entire overwhelming weight.

"Listen, boy," he grumbled, and shook his head with displeasure, "you must not get me wrong – but you know – I would not leave the stranger alone so much anymore with her, do you understand me?"

"With Lilli?" I asked slowly.

I was so prepared for it that I was hardly shocked, and yet it seemed to miserable me as if the old man had in this moment taken my heart between his calloused fists to crush the trembling thing.

"Yes, yes," Uncle Holm repeated reluctantly, "I don't know, Karl, you are so inexperienced in such a thing, probably also stuck too deep in your books. Look, my boy, the two seem to me a bit too familiar with each other. I don't want to frighten you, and it's probably also nothing, but such a young wife must always be protected by her husband. He must sometimes put the damned bridle on her, because the human nature of woman tends to such tricks, unfortunately God. I don't want to say anything further to you, and now you must act like a husband, Karl."

He hobbled away from me. But in the doorway, he turned around once more, and growled back, "But don't be frightened, my boy – you hear? – Good night!"

***

Thoughtless, as if sleepwalking, I stepped back into the hall. In all this time, I acted as if I could not completely come to my senses, as if I were only a watcher during all these events.

The pair were still standing by the fire, and warming their hands. While I looked, it occurred to me how gentle and winsome the lines of this bent female body were, and how rosily the flames had breathed over her usually so white countenance.

"Lilli," I cleared my throat loudly. "We should seek out our room; I'm tired."

She straightened up, and brushed her forehead as if she were returning into a hateful, disdainful world only at my call. Then her eyes sought those of the Captain, firmly and immersing, as if she wanted to express her thanks to him silently in this way for a happy hour.

I stood beside them, and did not stir. The numbness which had almost overwhelmed me previously on the yacht shackled my limbs anew.

Then they offered one another their hands, and then – he bowed, whilst wishing her "good night", to kiss her fingers.

Great God, don't let me think of it anymore! Something stabbed through me as if someone had bored through my throat with smouldering firebrands. I performed an instinctive movement. For at the time, at the time the desolate, blood-red thoughts first ambushed me which later lived off my life marrow, ranted and raved behind me, until finally that lust for annihilation had been lit in me which overcame me in the end.

How easily it could now have already occurred. He stood so inclined, bowing so deep – a hefty push from my hands, and the proud man would have tumbled into the gigantic, hissing stove.

I shuddered. It was the first time that such a monstrous idea had occurred to me.

"Come, Lilli," I demanded gruffly.

Then we went.

When she was walking next to me up the stairs, I had also made my decision. Now no quarter could be spared anymore, I had to get out of this turbidity.

The waiter led us to our room, and I was still watching my beautiful wife as she sat down exhausted at the table, and propped her head in her hands, dreaming to herself. A light was burning before her, and I walked up and down the small room several times uneasily.

Then Lilli pricked up her ear, and listened.

"Can you hear," she began, "Jensen is walking up and down next door. What a firm step he possesses, don't you think?"

Him again, nothing but the constant yearning thoughts of the stranger.

This one remark determined the rest of my life. I stopped before her, and slowly laid my hand on her shoulder. Instinctively she sank in the same way as if the touch were unpleasant to her.

Grinding my teeth, I had to experience that. We were thus spiritually and physically already separated. She felt physical repugnance when I stroked her. That robbed me of the remainder of my dignity and self-control.

"Lilli," I rose with a hoarse voice, while my chest was skimmed by the chill of a cold fever. "Isn't it time that we told the truth to one another, my child? Speak to me completely openly. Isn't it true that your soul no longer belongs to me, but to the man in there? In your heart, desires have been awoken which all urge you to the stranger. I know it. What shall happen with us now? But tell the truth, you see I am quite calm."

I was wanting to urge her still further when her hand touched me, and instinctively I started from the icy coldness streaming out of her fingers. In the shine of the flickering light, I noticed what a deathly pale colour her features had assumed. Her eyes were gazing unnaturally widened out of her distraught countenance at me. At first her lips just moved soundlessly, as if the blessing of speech had been robbed from her. Then she rose, and pressed both my hands beseechingly before her breast as if she wanted to shut up all further words by me there.

What she stammered to herself was barely comprehensible.

"Karl, what are you saying? — — My God, have you gone mad? — To me it seems — — through you, I am hearing and thinking something similar for the first time. — — Just how could you!" —

And suddenly she threw herself lengthwise on the chaise longue so that I could now see her only from the back, and her entire body shook and trembled as if a spasm were passing through this young body.

Then I stood, and grasped my forehead.

Was it really possible that I, madman, had just now pointed out to my white, delicate wife the sin which already towered silently and enormously behind her, just lying in wait for her to turn to it?

In the next moment, I was sitting by her side, and attempting to lift her up.

But she shook reluctantly like the first time. "Go," she cried sobbing, and now a tone of aversion sounded overtly.

"You should not touch me – go," she repeated once more.

Turned away from me, she remained lying for several more minutes, then she suddenly leapt up, all harsh and fitful, to place herself before the only window in our room. There she pressed her forehead against the panes, and stared out into the dreary night. How long I remained silently behind her, I do not know anymore, it must have been some time; she did not stir, I just heard sometimes how she groaned from the depths of her chest.

But in me it was climbing hot and tormenting. It seemed as if all my nerves were beginning to sing a wild song. I had the feeling quite distinctly that my thoughts were shifting, that I was no longer clear about my person and that which I had evoked in the moment.

"Lilli," I cried, suddenly fearful.

I still hoped she could turn, she could fly around my neck laughing and crying like before, it could turn out that everything had just been a confused, awful dream.

But she did not stir. Turned away, and divorced from me, the offended woman brooded to herself.

Was she really innocent? Or was her inner being outraged only thus rudimentarily because I had uncovered the innermost core of her being and exposed by it at the same time her unveiled, stained image?

I do not know what compelled me to once more make an attempt.

"Lilli," I murmured, while I approached her anew, daunted and half numb. "Lilli, I beg you from the bottom of the heart to speak the truth to me. Look, what I indicated before has been engaging me already for a long time. I am so horribly afraid that I — yes, why shouldn't I unburden myself of it — that my outward appearance seems to insignificant and unattractive to you, that the silence of our house has gradually become oppressive to you. — Is it that, Lilli? — I implore you, beloved child, be open with me."

I do not remember what else I murmured, begged, and implored. In the agitation, I lifted my hands, and began to embrace both her arms as if I wanted to draw her back to me.

And again — she shook reluctantly and horribly as if throwing off a caterpillar from her bare skin.

"Just go," she ordered once more, and in her voice lay so much coldness and deliberation that I noticed the inner decision had now fallen for her.

It had thus happened.

The axe had shattered the rosy red ribbon which my imagination had spun around me and around my ardently desired wife from the beginning. The ugly farce of the pitiful academic who conquered a goddess, and had wanted to force her to live in his dreary home, finished with shrill laughter.

Staggering, I crept out.

Down the corridor, I saw still half in a whirl the fur and clothes of Uncle Holm hanging. As I came past, I heard loud snoring. Then I knocked, loud and distinctly, until the old man finally opened his door for me in bewilderment.

"Karl!" he cried astonished, and when I ejected something incoherent, he drew me hastily into his room.

Yes, the farce was leaning towards its end — not yet fully, for the last words would be written blood-red and gleaming in the book of my life.

XV

This morning, my neighbour in the next cell was carried out; she had passed away in the night unnoticed.

Strange, what a silence now reigns next to me! I had become so accustomed to her songs and burlesque.

Now the clogs of the warders are clattering in there on the stone floor; it's being scrubbed, the windows are being opened, the last traces of this being are being washed from the walls with sharp essence.

I would have liked to have farewelled her. Now she has evaporated so quickly into the endless soul of the world.

"Go there," you little, treacherous, unneighbourly woman whom I became fond of in the course of years. Who will now sing your mischievous songs to me? And how long will I myself still live in my cage? – Who knows?

***

We travelled home from Putbus on the train. Touching were the awkward attempts of Uncle Holm to interrupt the icy silence which reigned between me and my wife by his harmless jokes, for the night which I had spent alone and without explanation with him spoke a comprehensible language for the old man, and made him apparently fear the worst for my ease.

Only Lilli did not react to anything. Pale and silent, she looked out the window at the passing landscape, and only occasionally directed a word at

Captain Jensen sitting opposite her, who naively strove to continue the conversation.

Before long, we arrived in our home town. Thank God! Now we could part.

Hastily I said goodbye to the other two, and hurried, as worn out even as I felt, immediately to the university so as not to neglect the advertised course of lectures.

Uncle Holm faithfully accompanied me, his bulky, fur covered arm shoved ponderously under mine.

"Boy," he suddenly said, and I heard the inner compassionate heartache seemingly arising from him, "you haven't reproached her perhaps? – Beware, Karl, that would be the stupidest thing you could do. Just don't speak a word more about it. Follow my advice, my boy, not a word more, you hear? The human creature forgets so easily. And the fellow running here will probably be fetched by the devil soon with God's help, if not elsewhere, then at the North Pole. – Just be sensible, Karl, and don't say anything. Promise me that, my boy, eh?"

He held his broad paw out to me, and I, hurt by every memory of what had occurred, constantly living only in images of that night past, only ever having before my eyes that appalling movement of aversion and tedium by my wife, I struck his right hand in the desire to part from him, and burst out in a rush, "Yes, yes, uncle – I will do everything – believe me – the whole thing is insignificant and dealt with. – – No, no, leave me, you see, I don't have any more time. – Adieu."

"Well, then so long," Uncle Holm growled, although I had already torn myself away. And when I was already far off in the inner courtyard of the university, the old man stood, in his massive boots and with the shaggy sheep's pelt, for a long time before the gates, shook his head, and spat distressed before himself.

***

With the mobilisation of all my powers, I had lectured to my students. Again I was only occupied by the thoughts. What would happen now? Would Lilli leave me? And why had I now left her alone? I was seemingly offering her the opportunity to stay with the stranger undisturbed.

I felt distinctly that I was lecturing my students with turbid, fuzzy stuff, unworthy to be taught by me — superfluous for them to hear.

Once more I was startled by it. What had become of me? How deeply had I sunk that I thus sinned against the spirit of my art and my scholarship? But the next moment robbed me again of clear reflection, wiped everything away.

Only my wife floated before me, my wife and the other man — the orphan whose dangerous merits I myself had brought to her attention on the ill-fated night, the orphan to whom I had perhaps now just pushed her with besotted hand.

My God, it seemed to me as if my brain would burst, as if a burning fluid were running around in infinite circles in my head.

For a long time, I could not bear it — and yet how pleasant it was to think of my breakup.

My father had also ended this way.

I walked home. Already from a distance, I could see the dear face of my mother waving to me from the double-sided spying mirror which was placed before her window so as to be able to comfortably peer down the street. Despite the heavy snowfall, the little woman hastily opened the window to call out to me.

What had happened? Had Lilli perhaps left my house already?

With a few leaps, I travelled up both the narrow wooden stairs so that I could step before my mother with gasping breath into the cosy room with the comfortable red mahogany furniture.

The little old woman was still sitting by the window, her lean face glowing with agitation. When she saw me enter, she lifted her hands up trembling towards me.

"Karl — Karl — just what has happened?"

"What — then — mother?"

"With Lilli — —"

"She hasn't — — nothing has happened to her though?" I cried.

At that moment, I was afraid of nothing so much as her death which I later yearned for avidly.

"No — no, but when I went down to her before — there — —"

"Well?"

"Think, she did not let me in there. She was sitting in her locked room, but I heard her sobbing loudly sometimes."

Concerned, I stared at the speaker.

Then the old woman rose, stood before me, and stroked my cheek softly. "Come, sit, my boy, here with me on the sofa — you haven't been up here with me in so long — and now tell me everything, my boy, that I don't know. Everything, okay?"

She stroked my hands and talked to me ever more urgently with her gentle, trembling voice.

"Don't be stupid, Karl, you won't want to keep any secrets from me, will you, my son? I have nothing left but you, you are the only thing left to me in this world. See, and then I'm living in your house too, and see and hear everything. And whoever does something to you, he violates me ten times more. But tell me now also, my boy, now tell also what burdens you. — — Now, so — Karl — come."

With her words, she had drawn me closer and closer to herself so that now my head rested almost on her chest.

I was again the small, delicate Karl, the sick, helpless child who had been nurtured like a hothouse plant under artificial temperature by this trembling, kindhearted woman.

Why had she not just let the pitiful germ which was so unsuited to life perish in due time, why?

"Now so — tell me, boy!"

"Because — — because — —"

A part of the old mood really came over me, a remnant of those childhood years when I had to entrust everything which excited me unconditionally to the small, white-haired woman, and when I felt that the old woman's cheeks were dampening, then I could not shut up my sorrow in myself any longer. I hid my head in both hands, and groaned loudly, "Mother — Lilli — has — no affection for me anymore."

"What?"

"She despises me."

"God in Heaven — — no, no." Then she shoved me away from her, and forcibly lifted up my head.

"Dear," she stormed, while her chest struggled for breath, "you are only imagining that, quite certainly. How can one not be fond of you anymore, think, Karl, when all people are so good to you; eh when – it would be laughable. You are my beloved, only child. Aren't you? – Tell me, how did you come upon this?"

But I did not give any more answers, instead brooding groaning to myself.

The old woman became more and more rushed, ever tenderer. I felt how her weak body trembled next to me.

"Karl," it came sparing from her lips, "you aren't thinking perhaps because of – Jensen?"

I let my hands fall, and stared at her for a moment.

Then the clever old woman understood.

Shaking she rose, and paced out the little room aimlessly and ringing her hands.

"My God – my God –" she stuttered, and the wrinkles in her countenance deepened, and seemingly travelled into each other, "that is surely not possible – Lilli is so loving – so loving. But I must get behind it. Of course. I will not let my child be made unhappy. Eh, where then – Karl, my boy, now you are here – you will surely be able to eat with your mother too? – And after dinner, yes, after lunch I'll go downstairs. And now, take your hands from your eyes. Karl, dear, you shouldn't do that, that I cannot bear to see."

She ran out to call the maidservant in, and in-between I had pulled myself together a little. My mother chattered constantly while she ran back and forth because of all her domestic duties, without letting me out of her eye. She constantly sought to distract my attention.

"Look, the fine large napkins. Do you remember? – Your father brought these back from Marseille. – And here's the silver ring for one – it is already a bit twisted, you bit into it once – yes, yes, Uncle Holm gave it to you as a godfather's present – and the golden Louis d'or. I still have it too."

She stroked me again over my hair. "And now come, Karl, – – roast veal – we haven't sat like this for a long time."

***

In the afternoon, my mother left me, and sought out my wife as she had indicated before.

I remained alone.

It could only have been a few minutes, but time stretched for me, like with all those who wait, into eternity.

For I was so frail that I actually still hoped, yes, wistfully assumed that a change could occur, that all this could only be a passing state.

In the corner, the big ancient grandfather clock ticked, my glance was caught by the colourful holy images of the metal clock face which had been looked at with astonishment by me in my childhood; only nothing could distract me.

Again and again, I had to listen for whether the old woman would not be returning soon from below.

And what message would she bring?

Oh, how shameful it was for me that I even needed an intermediary between me and my wife.

Finally the old woman came.

Around her mouth played a strangely bashful aspect, as if she were measuring me with an uncertain look.

"Mother, have you spoken to her?" I stammered.

And then the old woman broke forth falteringly and bashfully, that she had been received by Lilli, and encountered her this time quite calm too.

Admittedly, she would not give an answer to my mother's multiple questions. She had just squeezed the hand of the worried woman, and said after longer deliberation that mother could be quite at ease. She would give her husband, whom she expected soon, an explanation.

"An explanation?" I said, failing to understand.

"Yes, Karl," my mother said, "that was all. And now go, my son, and speak with her."

And while she stroked my softly on the sleeve, she said with face averted and half to herself, "The same happens in every marriage. You must not drive things to the brink, my boy. Just go, everything will certainly be okay again. — Just go."

XVI

The twilight had already set in when I stepped through the large stateroom, and disappeared into my study.

Timidly and sheepishly as if I did not belong there, I had crept through my own apartment on tiptoe.

When I thought of meeting with Lilli, my heart pounded like that of a ruined man who awaits a damning verdict from his judge.

For I had been discarded by her. That I knew.

Without clear emotion, I lit the copper lamp, and settled down at my desk as if I were thinking of working.

The great folio of the old monk from the Cistercian Abbey lay still untouched on the desktop.

The hopefully begun work had not progressed in days.

Mechanically, I leafed through the parchments; then I listened again for whether Lilli's soft steps would soon sound now.

The portière rustled, and I started. But it was only Professor Wackermann, whose sounds I must probably have ignored.

I greeted him monosyllabically, and so unjustly was I thinking already that I entertained the question to myself almost reluctantly: Must this old book stool disturb you just at the most inconvenient time? What interests you actually with this wizened visionary? And what concern to you basically is the surviving manuscript of the Cistercian monk who perhaps also only wrote in his joyless cell from weariness and boredom? — —

The Professor must have noted my mood, for he asked me quite cagily whether we would continue with our work now.

Remaining silent, I offered him a few translations which I had finished recently alone, and without his help.

The old man adjusted his blue glasses, and while I, distracted and agitated, sought to capture with aching ear every noise arising behind the portière, he skimmed the rhymes turned into German by me.

Has Lilli still not come?

How could I remove this old man, who obviously possesses neither the slightest feeling nor the least understanding for the stabbing sorrow which is destroying me within? –

Has Lilli still not come?

Still not? – Still not? –

Thus I slipped as Wackermann several times looked up from his sheet and shook his head thoughtfully.

Finally he placed the manuscript gently on the table, his entire figure collapsed, and as his dignified head with its grey hair almost touched the green desktop, he uttered restrainedly, and yet with affectionate reproach, “Karl, you won’t take this the wrong way?”

I was so impatient.

“What then?” I called sharply.

“You know, you cannot leave the poems standing here in this form. You must look through them once more.”

“Why then?” I called stiffly.

The old man looked up at me from below, and in his look lay something almost sorrowful, heavily aggrieved.

“Karl, I don’t know, but it is all so weak, so not at all like you were writing earlier. Boy, I think you should even draw back for some time from the work, for such a back step wouldn’t disrupt you in your youth. Do you understand?”

“Back step?” I murmured speechless, and at that moment, my heart began pounding loudly.

Even that as well? Was the halfheartedness which I had recently met with in the depths of my state of life taking vengeance already? Was the last dry clod on which I had stood until now also slipping from under my feet?

Suddenly I laughed out aloud.

"Karl, what is the matter with you?" the old gentleman cried shocked, and sprang up fearfully, but I had in my mood no consciousness that it was I myself who had laughed so shrilly, and hence just stared at the Professor with blanched cheeks.

"It's nothing," I endeavoured to get out, "I was a little indisposed those days; – believe me, dear friend, tomorrow I'll send you new poems – then you will see – – certainly. – – You weren't thinking" – at the same time, I pointed at the sheet that had just been put down – "that I was already done with these things?"

Wackermann was still shaking his head.

"No, Karl," he conceded in a soft voice, "I don't think that either."

"You will see," I nodded further in spasmodic excitement. "I am absolutely not worn out. Tomorrow you will see."

The old man walked up and down the room a few times, and brushed his hand over the bookcases along the wall as though in a soliloquy. Then he sat down again next to me, and gently closed the great folio which still lay open before me. Slowly he took it from the table, and put it under his arm.

"What are you wanting to do with the book?" I asked, taken aback.

Then he nodded as definitely as I had seldom seen the old man nod, and offered me his hand in farewell.

"No, boy," she concluded earnestly, "you should not stir here for the next few days. You are worth too much to me for that. And, in addition, our scholarship is also too sacred to me. — Nothing may be done incompetently. — I am taking the folio home with me. In a week, Karl, when you are again in a right place, we will speak further, God willing."

And without showing consideration for my distinctly recognisable consternation, for my begging outstretched hands, he nodded to me once more wordlessly, and I saw how deep shadows had sunk into his high forehead as if this noble soul had been clouded, or as if he were feeling heavy anguish over something precious, lost.

"Farewell, Karl," he wished me with his dear, tuneful voice.

He put on his slouch hat, pulled at his scarf, and stepped out the door slowly with the great folio.

I never saw it again.

Farewell, you dear old dreamer! — Your Karl has sinned no more against the scholarship which you call sacred.

I know you will have expedited my legacy with anguished heart and pure spirit.

You are the mild, believing priest, whilst I parted as fetish-man, as juggler and castoff.

Farewell!

***

I sat alone again.

The incisive doubt which Professor Wackermann had kindled in me passed through my head frighteningly.

If I was now really an outcast from the sacred temple of scholarship? What was still left to me then?

And again my thoughts strayed from these so serious things, and greedily fluttered around the image of my wife who did not want to approach.

Had Lilli deceived my mother?

Would this silence now last eternally between us?

But no, my sharpened ears suddenly perceived a rustling like Lilli's clothes tended to give, and slowly and ponderously, the covering was pulled back.

There she stood.

I was shocked at how pale and changed this beautiful creature looked. She again appeared to me like a wandering marble statue.

She sat down in her old armchair next to the stove, and slowly stroked the tiles with her hands as if she were freezing.

Then, when she noticed how expectantly and anxiously she was embraced by my look, she spoke calmly and clearly, yes, really with a thought-out decisiveness.

"Karl, I told your mother that I have something significant to share with you."

She leant back, and looked steadily at me. "I have considered it properly, quite clearly. By you yourself, it was pointed out to me, and I have not learnt to lie. You also have the right to learn my innermost thoughts."

"Lilli," I cried appalled, and sprang up completely numbed. "It isn't true? The frightful thing can't be true? Well?"

She did not lower her large, clear eyes, but continued to follow me with them. "Yes, it is true," she replied definitely, and sighed deeply. "I could not myself imagine it – but it is true. – It seems to me as if yesterday you had just perfectly solved a puzzle for me which I would never have solved myself."

"So I?" I cried painfully.

But she continued as if I had not spoken, "Yes, Karl, I was struggling with myself — today — for the entire day, I have fought against these thoughts as if they were bringing a sickness. I recalled to my mind all the kindness and love that I felt continually for you. But nothing helps, nothing. You yourself have now opened the door for these awful thoughts, and they are coming through unhindered. I recognise thereby that my innermost nature is accessible to you, yes, even calls to you."

She spoke so calmly, but I broke down from the few words as if heavy crushing blows were meeting my head.

"And so here ends everything between us?" I groaned in agony. "Now is everything over?"

"Over?" she repeated, and looked at me with her large, dark eyes.

"Yes, Karl, I wanted to ask you just that, and hence I am forced to place the truth before you. See, it seems constantly to me as if a tremendous, not so numbing voice calls and shouts with every power after the stranger of whom I hardly know anything. It seems to me as if I had known him an eternity, yes, as if I had never been separated from him. I believe in such tempers that he is a part of my body which I cannot at all do without. But it is so strange — and in it exists the woeful, the conflicting thing which I feel, it is not a loving and warm voice which calls me to him; — it seems constantly to me as if it does not come from the heart at all. It seems to me as if it were only my limbs which draw me constantly to him, and it is just that, this physical urge which scares me, and yet which I cannot overcome."

"No," I murmured whilst the unattractive, the diminutive, the insignificant parts of my person were shattered before the eyes of my broken self. "You will not overcome it, it will certainly urge you more and more – oh God, Lilli. – Why must it be? – Why?"

"Why?" she shrugged her shoulders. "That I don't know, I only know – and now listen carefully, Karl – that my nature and my mind command me constantly that I must subjugate this improper, and certainly also impure desire! And I certainly will subjugate it," she spoke further, breathing deeply; "only, Karl" – and here her tone lost something of its previous hardness – "only you must spare me, not question, not torment, and be lenient with what seems to you weakness in me. See, it is perhaps a sickness with which I struggle, and which wants to have its time. Don't you think? Will you promise me that?"

With that she rose, and stretched her hand out to me with one of her beautiful movements.

She was so clear, so proud, so quite without shame, so completely convinced that it was only about a natural expression of her life.

Truly, how narrow and timid I seemed opposite her, how boxed in by all sorts of scholarly notions, how oppressed by countless moral teachings which I never questioned.

Hesitantly I laid my fingers in her outstretched right hand. My soul was torn up, my strength of will not strong enough to reach a clear decision.

And yet I offered her my hand.

"We will of course limit our social interaction with Jensen to the barest minimum," my wife continued with her unnatural calm and stiffness. "He will then soon note the change and its cause. I will also speak to him once more myself today."

"You – want to – speak to him ...?"

"Yes, I want to see him once more," she insisted firmly.

And as she stepped closer to me, and almost lovingly placed both her hands on my shoulders, she concluded with softly trembling voice, "Now you know everything, Karl. You won't make it difficult for both of us, will you? You possess such a tender, sympathetic soul like hardly any other man has, and the likes of which I certainly could not do without."

"And yet? – – and yet, Lilli?" I suddenly sobbed loudly.

She drew her hands back from me.

"Now stop that," she ended again clear and definite, and while I collapsed groaning at my desk, the portière rustled, and my wife was no longer with me.

XVII

Two hours later, I was running through the dark streets. The evening had already sunk over the town; the mild weather had begun; cold damp mist had crept from the sea, and was surging through the dimly lit lanes.

I saw and felt hardly any of that.

The single driving wish which seethed hot and overpowering in my breast consisted of finally settling with the stranger.

Yes, that was it. I had to know and learn how it stood for me, for my name, for my house, and for my honour.

Lilli had spoken so coolly and coldly, without also wanting the suspicion to arise that ruin had already drawn her into its arms, that the sin had already taken power over her.

It had all been sins of thought, follies of the heart, greedy desires. At least I thought I had understood her thus.

But if I was deceiving myself? If this white divine image had already been worn down, eaten away at by the caustic acid of wickedness?

My God, the air faltered in me, the black mist penetrated tormentingly into my lungs until I thought I would suffocate.

No, I had to speak to him.

There already existed a torturous delight in it for me to see the enemy who had stolen my rosy treasure, and to graze on his embarrassment.

Ever more avidly, I paced out the streets. Once it seemed to me as if I saw the bearish figure of Uncle Holm hobbling past me, I even believed I heard a call, but I pushed my coat collar still higher, and hurried past wordlessly.

Soon I found myself before the Steinbeck gates, where the houses became smaller and more and more like little fishermen's and farmers' huts. Here lived Jensen.

It was a small, low house whose shingle-clad roof rose not far above a man's height from the ground. The green window shutters were already closed, cosy, yellow light only came through the heart shaped notches.

When the planked door opened, a faint tinkle sounded first of all. Then I stepped across a brick paved hallway, and finally knocked on the low door behind which Jensen lived.

No answer.

Heavy fear crept over me that he might not be home.

Once more I pounded, then I opened the door cautiously, and stepped timidly into the small, narrow room which was lit cosily by a simple floor lamp.

While I looked around the lonely apartment, a strong, bearish woman appeared with clattering clogs, whom it was to be noted must have just been cleaning the little house.

"Are you wanting our Captain?" she inquired, and propped both arms on her sides.

I affirmed that.

"He isn't here. But he may come back soon."

"Then I will wait."

"Well good, that you do."

With that, she clattered out again.

Exhausted, I settled down on the simple green sofa which flaunted a few crocheted covers, and observed with faint interest the modest furniture of my opponent. On the table before me lay all sorts of nautical instruments: compasses, thermometers, a telescope, and a few large microscopes for inspecting plants. With envy I realised how far the interests of this man extended.

In the corner of the room, close to the window, a piano stood with sheet music open on it. I knew that Jensen was a deep and passionate admirer of music.

But my awful thoughts did not let me linger for long on such ideas.

Where would Jensen likely be found now? Perhaps he was right at this moment with her, right now when I, as if in scorn, was sitting in his deserted room waiting for the robber of my happiness.

Outside the thunderstorm blew harder against the wooden shutters. On the roof of the house, it began to mutter and whistle, a heavy draught came out of the stove.

Whether I should start again?

Then heavy steps crunched over the flagstones, an energetic hand struck at the door knocker, and, enveloped deep in his blue mariner's coat, the gold laced cap on his head, the tall figure of my host appeared in the doorframe.

He had to stoop as he walked in.

"Ah?" he emitted surprised. "Professor?"

In his honest features, a tremendous embarrassment began to work. It occurred to me how tired, colourless and slack the otherwise so freshly animated face of the man looked today.

My unexpected visit seemed to rob him completely of his entire confident manliness, and to put him from the outset at a disadvantage opposite me.

Remaining silent, he took off his coat, opened a cupboard, and placed glasses and a bottle of wine down before me. Then he brought out a bundle of large, foreign cigars, lit himself one, and remained standing by the table with tilted forehead and lowered eyes as if he were seeking a beginning.

Now was right.

I had to not let him have a minute to think, I thought to act by surprise. I wanted him off the top of his head to confirm his unholy affection for my wife.

Only it happened differently.

He blew a few thick clouds of smoke out, breathed out deeply so that it almost sounded like a sigh, and suddenly riveted his grey eyes clearly and penetratingly on me.

"Professor," he began with visible restraint, while I began trembling with surprise and astonishment, "I have just come from your wife."

"From where?" I whispered.

The openness was inconceivable, it smashed and shattered all the plans which I had been devising so cleverly up to now.

"Yes, I come straight from her," he repeated, and again stared down at the table before him, unmoving.

Then I pulled myself together. "Were you seeking me in my house?" I choked out hoarsely, stressing the word "me" strongly.

"No."

"Whom then?"

"I was taking leave from Lilli — — taking leave from your wife."

"From Lilli?"

He fell silent, and looked incessantly down before him at the red tablecloth.

"You were taking leave?" I repeated half unconsciously.

"Yes."

He behaved as monosyllabically as if he had to tear each word from his soul, as if it all hurt him physically. His lowered forehead darkened, and wrinkled even more. The man seemed to be visibly suffering.

It remained silent between us for a fairly long while. You could only hear the beating of the rain and, from outside, the loud howling of a steam whistle ringing out from the harbour.

Then Jensen slowly offered me his hand, and let it fall again after some time when he perceived that I did not want to notice this salutation.

"I would also like to say goodbye to you now, Professor," he said, forcing himself to be calm with all his might, "for I will be departing already in three days."

Then something shot through my head.

"Your expedition, Captain," I smiled suddenly with wild joy, "your journey starts, as far as I know, not for two months; — you have then surely made the decision for your hasty departure quite suddenly?"

He nodded. "Yes."

"Just today?"

"Yes, Professor."

"So? And we both won't see you again after this?"

"With God's help not."

He was quite open.

Opposite this great truthfulness, the courage to ask yet more abandoned me. What else did I want to hear? It all lay so distinctly before me, as if this taciturn man had handed over a comprehensive confession.

It was almost written legibly on his forehead, “It drives me away because the sin is already flying over me with its black wings, and because it will in short time hold me in its claws if I do not flee unhesitatingly from it.”

Hence the sudden journey.

Once more I raised my eyes to him, once more I impressed on myself this tall, muscular figure who still stood with lowered head by the table, so firmly that it has remained indelibly fastened in my memory so that it still follows me even now as I write this.

Then I straightened up, and stepped without saying anything, not even giving him a word of farewell, quickly out of his house.

In the hallway, I paused for a while, and listened, but as much as I strained my hearing, it all remained still in the little room. The Captain seemed to still linger motionless by the table as if he did not want to tear himself away from the dismal thoughts which surrounded him there.

***

“Jensen was with me barely after you had left the apartment.”

It was the first word that Lilli directed at me when, in the evening, I stepped wet-through into the dining room where she waited by the set table.

We were both alone, my mother decided not to disturb us this day, but to leave us time for the reconciliation which, as she thought, had already begun between us.

"I know that he visited you," I replied, while I sat down outwardly calm at the table. – Oh, how this restraint robbed me of the last powers which were still flowing in my crushed body. – "I spoke to him as well."

She started. "You did, Karl?" she inquired.

"Yes, I spoke to him when he returned from you."

"And so you also know now that he is leaving us inside three days?" she continued less certainly, and I saw how something like a trace of restrained anguish ran over her pale countenance.

"Yes, Lilli," I replied, keeping to myself, "he revealed the lot to me."

We did not speak with one another for a few minutes.

With lowered eyelashes, she seemed to be considering, then she suddenly offered me her hand across the table, and while I grasped it with bleeding heart and yet avidly, she asked me, "Are you at peace now, Karl?"

I wanted to stammer out a 'yes', only I was incapable of it. And the expression in my eyes must have been so bleak and torn up, and so much ruefulness must have been reflected in my entire being that it even attracted my struggling wife's attention, and she asked me with softly quivering voice, "Karl, do you wish to learn something else? You know that I don't conceal anything from you."

"Yes, Lilli," I whispered abruptly to her, and suddenly kissed ardently and urgently those little fingers which still rested in my hand, although I noticed how painfully they trembled at the same time. "I beg you, would you still confide in me how you parted from

Jensen? You must sympathise with me that it torments me and does not allow me any rest."

Then she withdrew her right hand, and propped her head in both hands as if she could not bear the strange and contradictory thing any longer.

"That you shall also learn," she looked up haggardly. "I told him everything openly, and begged him to go before it was too late."

"You did that?" I cried. "Now, and he? – and he, Lilli? Now tell me the truth."

She smiled bleakly. "He said almost nothing. He just nodded gently in agreement with my words as if I were demanding something quite obvious, and then —"

"Now – and then?" I trembled all over.

"Then" – an abrupt blush flew over her cheeks, she sank her head deeper, and spoke the following as quietly to herself as if she herself wished her words would die away and flutter off unheard.

"Then he drew me to himself, without violence, quite calmly, and kissed me, without any excitement, so quietly, so earnestly, as if this weren't the first caress which he had ever allowed himself. Shortly after that, he strode out the door with a strong squeeze of my hand, and without saying anything."

She fell silent.

I did not speak another word either, I just rose mechanically and ponderously, and clamped my hand to my forehead.

No, no, it was no illusion; this last revelation, this appalling image of my wife lying in his arms, this last scene playing back and forth with such illuminating, colourful, glowing colours before me – it all certainly seared my brain with its sparkling lights.

Something was twitching and storming under my hair that I could not subjugate anymore, I felt quite distinctly that I was in this moment no longer master over my thoughts.

XVIII

The next day, I had my lectures cancelled. I was sick, really sick, and lay feverish and chilled on the chaise longue of my little room, and attempted to distract my desolate thoughts through reading.

No, not only remaining stuck to these appalling thoughts on which I had been caught like the buzzing fly on flypaper, not constantly brooding over this one incident playing in thousands of colours of how she lay in his arms and was kissed by him — ardently, urgently and insolubly, as she had certainly never been kissed before.

Away, away! — Why are you tormenting me, you stabbing, treacherous thoughts? Why don't you leave me in peace? — I only want to have peace and distraction.

I am always tearing new books from the shelves, and piling them up before me, quite aimlessly, just as they fall into my hand.

Meanwhile all the devils of suspicion are conspiring against me, to hound me, and pinch me with glowing tongs. Why else does a gloating kobold play the book of Tristan and Isolde straight into my hands, that incomparable love song of Master Gottfried of Strasbourg which also dispenses at the same time the bitterest song of scorn for cheated and all too patient husbands?

My heightened senses naturally recall in the sharpest manner that place which I can relate to myself. With trembling hands, I look it up. Where do the biting rhymes stand which show the suspicious, jealous and yet constantly cheated on King Mark in his entire glory?

Right, here I have them, and with lust, I slurp the consuming poison into me.

It stands:

The king asks with serious mind:
Where does she sleep, the queen?
They point him to the garden.
Then he went from the women
To see his heartbreak:
There lay his nephew and his wife,
One body next to the other
Huddled close in sweet union,
Cheek on cheek, mouth on mouth.
At their upper ends
The arms and hands,
Breast and shoulder, he saw
Everything had been so closely
Pressed and united;
And if a work had been poured
From bronze, from gold firm and tight,
Truly, it could not have yielded
More beautifully one to the other.
Thus the lovely couple slept
In full course, deep and sweet;

Not knowing of what they were weary.
— — Now, when King Mark sees there
His calamity openly before him,
Then what he so often desired was
Now all granted to him at base,
Now he had no need of doubt,
He saw before himself living death.

Yes, that was me, living death was also devouring me and creeping ever closer to my heart. In fact, I felt that I could not look down as calmly as the English king at the embracing couple. No, in me something else was stirring. Unobserved, it had enlarged, and was now pushing and kicking its way to the surface. Certainly, I had to defend myself, take revenge. Even the fever which was circling in my veins gave me no peace anymore and no respite for reasoned deliberation.

A voice was whispering ceaselessly in my brain, derisive and venomous, "King Mark! — King Mark! How do you know that you have not been cheated on for a long time? That it is not all a pack of lies to make you completely secure? Who gives you the guarantee that this grandiose openness of the two, before which you have shown so much awe, that it is not just the subtlest of traps which you have awkwardly drawn yourself into? Be alert, King Mark! He still remains another three days. What cannot occur in these three days? How much love cannot be savoured in these three days? For the day is followed by the night, the discreet night, the maid and panderer to all loving. And you, King Mark, are barred from such joys — from delicate sense, you remain distant from your wife. Awake, awake, clever King Mark, in three days your crown can probably become a legacy. – Liven up!"

No, I could not bear it any longer. With the fervour of the fever, I hurled the song of Tristan into the corner. In the same moment, the door opened, and in came my mother and Lilli who jointly remained sitting by my bed the entire morning. They covered me up, attempting to bring me into a sweat. My mother had already prepared all sorts of lemonades, and Lilli also asked from time to time how she could relieve my condition. But I just shook my head, and stared fixedly at her.

Thus this morning, I thought to myself, she was alone. This morning at least, she kept her promise not to see the ill-fated orphan again. But perhaps she had agreed with him on another hour. Perhaps in a discreet place – far outside the gate, perhaps in his own apartment. Oh, if only my mother had gone away; but the old woman remained sitting assiduously by my bed, and so I could exchange only perfunctory words with my wife.

The fever began to surge hotter and hotter through my body, my teeth chattered in my mouth, and yet I felt with a strange comfort how my courage and energy grew by the hour. It was as if the morbid fervour had ignited the life's fire which just smouldered so weakly in me into brightly blazing flames.

In the afternoon, the old woman finally left us to lie down to rest for a bit in her own apartment. I had to make use of this time. Begging, I grasped Lilli's hand, and began to agonise and implore.

"Isn't it true, Lilli, that you are thinking of your promise? Isn't it true, beloved child, I can rely firmly on it?"

She turned her head away from me, and nodded reluctantly. She apparently held this reminder to be indelicate and weak.

But I was incapable of acting otherwise. Every subtlety, every consideration had given way before the burning torment which was chafing me.

"And isn't it true, Lilli, you will not leave the house during these three days?" I continued. "That at least, you must allow me for my reassurance. Well? You will do that?"

It seemed to me anew as if a distinct sign of tedium was gliding around her twitching mouth, and yet she said succinctly, "If it seems right to you, then it shall be so too. But now, Karl, let all that rest, I begged you for that just yesterday."

Oh, I knew why she demanded silence from me anew. I should not even give his name, the beloved name for whose bearer she was pining away.

"You should not abuse the name of the Lord, your God!" Haha, I would have liked to have giggled aloud. Isolde was sitting by the bed of her sick sponsor, and yearning for her Tristan.

A consuming fury climbed in me. I would have liked to have lashed out in powerless rage that I should be so visibly and continually mocked, betrayed, and deceived.

I watched Lilli wordlessly for quite some time, and then — then it climbed up in me for the first time; an uncanny delight beset me with the thought, "If this women were to lie dead before you, then you would be single and rid of all the worrying; death is the actual lover she needs, he will hold her fast and guard her."

I suddenly pressed both hands over my eyes to get away from it, for my entire soul shuddered.

"Lilli, tell me something," I begged.

I wished for nothing more ardently than to be separated from this blood-red image.

But Lilli felt no propensity for chatting with me now, and so I continued brooding. Ever anew I had to look at her and imagine how she would surely look if I were to lay her out.

And with what would I condemn her?

Of course, there on the table before me sparkled the dagger which her lover himself had brought me, and which I had used before for cutting open tacked together books. It lay there, and the red ruby eye of its handle squinted across to me.

Horror seized me.

"Lilli, I beg you, speak to me!" I cried in my madness. Only my wish seemed just to provoke her contrariness, for she rose, and stepped towards the door.

"I'm too tired myself, Karl," she said dismissively, "and it's better for you if you remain alone now for a bit."

With that she disappeared behind the portière.

What a heartless, terrible crime, leaving me now with my red thoughts! I threw the covers from myself, straightened up, and crept to my desk. Like a desperate man, I struggled and battled with the fatal intentions which were stabbing me incessantly like a swarm of venomous insects.

Oh God, have mercy on me! A little sympathy!

Dully I brooded by my old place before me. Here before had lain the great folio that had also been stolen from me, or rather, that had been made safe from me. I was just no good for anything anymore.

Or did the entire affliction which enshrouded my head only exist because the deceitful woman lived by my side? Would the black fate which stepped closer and closer to me perhaps have disappeared if I had distanced her from me?

And again it seemed to me as if on the handle of the dagger sparkling behind me the great eye of the idol was opening to blink across at me penetratingly and encouragingly.

This one appalling idea was not leaving me.

"If it is possible that you were constantly deceived and lied to," so it hissed in me, "if she really only had a mind for coarse and brutal delights, then take her away. Then condemn her for fumbling with sinful hand on your honour, then don't spare her any longer, then cheat the other man from having her white body! How cosily warm her blood will trickle over your fingers and wash away from you all the anguish which you have suffered from her. How beautiful it would be if you could tear her out from the midst of her courtship, and have your vengeance."

At the same time, I shook with contradictory delight, and the evil ruby eye incessantly squinted across at me maliciously.

XIX

A day had passed. One of the three had finally rolled around. On the morning of the second, Professor Wächter appeared in my room, the famous psychiatrist, the same one who now keeps me unrelentingly captive in my cell.

The women had called for him behind my back because of my excited state.

He sat down by me, and began quite harmlessly to chat with me, and yet I noticed how his black eyes observed me tensely at the same time. That confused me even more. In the end, he shook my hand sympathetically, and forcefully recommended rest and relaxation.

"We have overstrained our nerves a bit too much, dear Professor," he tossed out in a chatty tone, "so ceasing work for a period and lots of going for walks, understand?"

I rocked back and forth uncomfortably in my chair.

"Yes, yes," I finally wrung from myself, "my father also suffered from such feverish apparitions. Could such a thing be hereditary?"

The psychiatrist turned back by the door once more, and threw an astonished look at me.

"No," he then comforted me finally, "you can be completely easy in your mind. Only much rest, you hear?"

With a friendly salutation, he went away, and immediately afterwards, Uncle Holm shoved himself through the door. He was carrying in his large gloves a small bouquet of white snowdrops which he stretched out towards me triumphantly.

“There, Karl,” he wheezed, “they are the first. The beasts almost curled up from that ice. I brought them with me to you for your cheer and delight.”

He sat himself down before me on a chair with legs apart. “Now tell me, how goes it with you?”

Wistfully I pressed my face into the bouquet; perhaps this first greeting of the coming spring could drive away the wild thoughts which were circling destructively in my brain.

“Karl, you look bad though,” Uncle Holm opined in his usual unhurried way. “The devil knows, it seems to lie in the air. I met Jensen before, who looks just as miserable. Yes, right, Jensen,” he paused, “what I wanted to tell you, Karl; he departs now the day after tomorrow, to Hamburg to start with. Now you see, my boy, that’s just as I told you. Now the entire thing has flown from your head.”

The kindhearted old man sat for almost an hour opposite me, and told every possible story from the town, and from the surrounding districts as well, which he thought could interest and excite me. But finally he felt probably that rest was most needed by me, and in the end, he hobbled humming and grumbling about the doctor out of my study.

Then I was alone again – alone with myself and my evil thoughts.

When my mother visited me, I asked after Lilli.

“Why doesn’t she come to me a little?”

And the old woman replied that my wife had some errands to do in town.

Embittered, I flared up, “She has really gone out?”

"Yes, of course," my mother replied, taken aback, "she must enjoy a bit of fresh air. Look, my son, how the sun already shines through the window."

Yes, spring was in the air, but my dismal mind slid down more and more into night and darkness. I continued brooding.

She had thus not kept her promise; she, who usually always deemed her word sacred, had broken it this time, and had escaped from the house. Oh, I knew it, I had immediately guessed it. However much I implored, whatever I suggested and asked for, it still drew her all-powerfully to him. Barely listened to, my words had died away before her. Isolde must huddle against her Tristan as long as he still dwelt here.

"Karl, is it getting worse for you?" my mother asked worriedly.

Yes, yes, it is getting worse for me, much worse; everything was twitching and leaping in me, I felt like I was no longer lord over the tiniest bone of my body.

What happened to me in the following hours, I do not know anymore.

I remember only darkly that I lay stretched out on my chaise longue, and played with the Mexican weapon which I now considered my only pleasure.

How strangely the sun reflected in the red ruby. It was almost as if the eye were laughing delightedly at me.

Thus I drifted for hours. Occasionally I thought thick grey mist was streaming into the room. And then I thought I saw all sorts of images and figures weaving up and down in the clouds. Strange! Strange! These images formed themselves more and more distinctly. I could have sworn I saw my father, in his skipper's uniform, and with his pale, uncanny countenance, striding through the room, and then it was again a monk carrying before him the great folio which I would translate.

The sweat flowed in streams from my pores. Towards evening, the fever abated, and when the lamp was lit, my wife also appeared by me. In vain, I hoped she would tell me of her trip, but she ignored all my hints with beaming silence as if she did not understand my agitation.

Oh certainly, certainly, she had been with him again. Who knows what exuberant fondling she had tolerated and dispensed. For truly, this woman must have been able to please. Only now did I realise it with my feverish eyes just for that reason. Her cheeks, which had seemed so pale and ghostly yesterday, were reddened tenderly again today, her eyes beamed again that beguiling dark blue.

No, I would not be deceived anymore, I would not be hoodwinked by anything any longer, not even by her tenderness suddenly surging up. For the figure of my wife unexpectedly bent over me, and slung both her arms around my weary shoulders.

"Karl," she whispered, "just get better again quickly for me, that is now my only wish; you will not punish me so hard, will you?"

And then she cuddled up to me so that I could feel all her soft limbs, and she kissed me tenderly on both eyes; a tear fell at the same time onto my countenance.

Then I lay, and closed my eyes out of desperation, faintness, and the drilling pain of knowing.

What should I believe? What should I hope?

"King Mark," it screamed in me, "be alert!"

***

Thus the last day dawned.

That black day in which the sun plunged down from my heaven, when all around me perished.

It was in the morning. Lilli was with my mother and I in the dining room. We were reading the paper while the old woman, busy with her knitting, sat by the window.

A peaceful stillness lay over the room. The sunlight was falling through the lowered curtains, and painting the pattern of the fabric on the floor.

From the rooves opposite, we could hear the melting snow dripping down, and the falling drops were sparkling in the sunlight like little balls of gold and silver.

Quite some time passed like that. From the tower of nearby St Nicholas, the bells reported the eleventh hour.

I still hear the mighty blows rolling through the air, for it was the tolling of the burial of my being, the death tolls for my entire existence.

And in the same moment, Lilli became restless. As I had been observing her constantly from behind my paper, I could detect that she was only giving the appearance of reading the paper. She was impatient, she threw inquiring glances at my mother and me, as if she thought herself unobserved, and then looked furtively at the grandfather clock by the wall.

The hand moved unceasingly. She seemed to be in a hurry.

I sat there, but no movement escaped me. Finally Lilli rose, and while she seemingly indifferently pulled the paper together, she said ingenuously to my mother, “I still have such a dull, occupied head, and since the weather is so bright, I'd like to walk in the open air again a little."

And with a gentle turn, she added, "Will you perhaps accompany me, Karl?"

At the same time, she did not look at me, and I had the distinct feeling that this question had only been tossed out to reassure me, and deceive me all the more completely.

Seemingly inattentive, I shook my head, "No, no, my child, I'll remain with mother."

"Well, as you will. I'll be back in an hour."

So in an hour. She seemed to lay no value at all on having promised me to leave our house during these three days under no circumstances. She acted as if those words had not fallen between us at all.

She calmly left the room, and returned again after some time in her winter attire to take leave of me and my mother. She offered her hand to us both with her usual steadiness.

Oh, how I secretly envied this purposeful woman. With a sort of timid admiration, I let her start on her way, although I knew that she would be strolling within an hour through that dark gate which permits no return.

"Goodbye, mama! Good day, Karl!" she tossed back gently once more.

Then I was alone with my mother.

The peaceful stillness which did me so well was again reigning in the wide room. The sun was painting its flower pattern before my feet like before, and the gold and silver balls were falling loud and ringing from the rooves onto the street.

Was it possible that in this idyll a man was sitting who sought his greatest ambition in shortly being a murderer?

Today this entire state seems inconceivable to me.

My heart did not beat an atom faster than usual. The fever had passed from me completely. I could have sat at my desk then and performed the most difficult work with fullest deliberation. Never had my mind been clearer, my thinking brighter. Strangest of all, however, it seems to me today that I did not entertain any speculation over my deed anymore. It seemed simple to me, as if I had to execute it, as if my undertaking were precisely as simple as throwing a badly selected book into the wastepaper basket.

When my wife had been gone for perhaps five minutes, I expressed the wish to my mother of likewise enjoying the fresh air a little; and when the old woman asked why I had not accompanied Lilli, I replied that I would attempt to catch up with her.

Hastily I then threw myself with her approval into my fur, and put on my top-hat as if I were going to a celebration. Then I offered my mother my hand, all without the certain feeling that it involved a farewell to life and death, and took myself into my work room once more as if by chance. There on the desk lay the Mexican weapon which at that moment, I considered my best friend. I quickly pocketed it, and stepped hastily down the stairs.

Now I found myself on the street. Immediately I set out through side streets on the way which had to lead to the house of Captain Jensen. And precisely after I had reached the harbour almost doubly quick, I discerned some distance from me the figure of my wife walking quite slowly, even hesitantly.

So I had not deceived myself.

Now caution was called for. I pressed myself close by the houses, and likewise checked my pace as if I were on a harmless stroll.

Lilli alone did not turn back. She seemed to be following her path indecisively, even reluctantly.

But not the slightest anxiety penetrated me, all fear had escaped from me, a clarity surrounded me which continually amazed me. I constantly had the feeling as if I were executing something thought up by someone else. And as I stepped out onto the main road into the midst of the bright sunlight, my entire being slid past me once more with complete clarity. It was thus the naturally necessary end for the shut-off, harmless man of books who did not know life or woman, and whom an oppressive fear had prevented from fathoming both with love. The fear, however, only lived so powerfully in him because he expected to be rejected by both, by life as well as the woman, and because he knew that they both mocked the thick film of dust which lay over him.

Now the same man found himself on the path to carrying out something again which life certainly did not support.

Here all my deliberations broke off, for Lilli executed a turn, and now found herself perhaps still thirty steps away from the house of her beloved. Now it was proven.

Should I really complete it?

For a moment, the blood shot into my temples. For a fleeting moment, it hammered in my brain so that I thought someone was pounding on my skull with iron fists. But then everything again became calm and clear around me.

Now it called for waiting to see what she would do.

My wife did not turn. Pensive, she remained standing by the low, green wooden fence, and plucked thoughtfully a few of the thin, bare twigs which shot up there. Then she again strolled on a few steps almost listlessly.

Five more steps to Jensen's door.

And then – then I discovered unexpectedly that he was himself standing at the window, and peering out.

Oh – so he apparently expected her.

She executed one more step.

That was her last.

He expected her – he expected her. To me it seemed as if an urgent signal blared before my ears.

Everything flowed together over me and into me like in a grandiose, tremendous melody. I heard the wailing of bells before my ears. The swishing of the sea over my head like a drowning man. The earth trembled and swayed under my feet. As if to save myself, I grasped for the dagger in my pocket, and lifted it high above me in the air.

I sprung over the lurching ground at her. She let out a loud scream.

For a second long, it still seemed to me as if I might just as well have plunged over her and suffocated her with my kisses.

Then a blue bolt of lightning. – A sputtering redness surrounded me, and it was all finished.

XX

Could it really be the truth? I have battled so long against it, now my strength to oppose it any longer has almost vanished. And I am beginning to believe.

I also have no ambition anymore, not even the ambition to have been the avenger of my honour.

Not even that.

***

For many months, I have not written any more in this book.

Limp and faint, I have been lying for weeks in my bed, and Professor Wächter is doing everything to make my stay in his elegant madhouse comfortable.

***

Could it really be the truth, what he tells me already so often, that, at the time by the garden fence, nodding over the bare azaleas, I had been attacked by a terrible brain fever, and that I had left the solitary act of my life undone just as I had been leading it up to its climax?

Professor Wächter says I had raised a dagger high over my wife in a blind frenzy, and had then collapsed suddenly before her, as though struck by lightning, and been carried away by Captain Jensen.

The next day, I had found myself here in the convivial house of the psychiatrist.

***

He speaks so insistently to me, the man with the face of Christ.

Oh woe, I am beginning to believe Lilli lives. And I, I am the dead one.

The one who passed away in his weakness.

***

I hear my wife appears almost every second day at the institute to inquire about my health. Always in the same black clothes which I know so well on her. Professor Wächter says her father has died, and she still lives quietly in our mariner's house, only engaged in the care for my ailing mother.

Uncle Holm also endeavours to come by frequently. He is a welcome guest with the assistant doctors to whom he openly expresses his derision.

But I do not want to see my life again.

They should not sympathise with me in my helplessness.

***

Nothing more has been heard of Jensen. – The northern land has swallowed him up.

***

I believe I will die.

Yesterday I dreamt about it. Then it seemed to me as if I had lifted myself from the grave of the mattress and walked up an endless mountain, into ever purer air, into ever more radiant brightness. And above, high above in azure blue, two figures towered up, a monk who held an enormous folio in his raised hands like Moses, and at his feet my wife huddled with her unfettered blond hair, raising her dark eyes religiously to him. Behind both figures, however, the sun's monstrous disc stood immovably so that both bodies seemed as though painted on a gold ground.

Sacred! Sacred!

And the monk read with loud voice the ancient verse from the book:

> Scholarship and art
> Are the grace of God,
> Are white and pure,
> Demand a life quite alone.

Then I stood and folded my hands devoutly. Yes, now I know that was the lost content of my life. I will die.

Selah!

About the Publisher

Our mission is to provide translations into English of the complete works of neglected major European writers. We do not cherry-pick works that seem the most marketable, but rather seek to provide a complete collection of each writer's works so that readers can follow the writer's development and decide on its merits for themselves.

http://www.facebook.com/KANitzPublishing

http://www.kanitzpublishing.com

www.ingramcontent.com/pod-product-compliance
Lightning Source LLC
LaVergne TN
LVHW101940220826
846093LV00006B/68

* 9 7 8 0 4 7 3 2 8 2 3 0 1 *